2011 B☑ P9-DIW-725

WITHDRAWN

TRY, TRY AGAIN

Other books by Julie Stone:

Déjà Who?
These Darn Heels

TRY, TRY AGAIN

•

Julie Stone

AVALON BOOKS
NEW YORK

Published by Avalon Books,
an imprint of Thomas Bouregy & Co., Inc.
160 Madison Avenue, New York, NY 10016

Library of Congress Cataloging-in-Publication Data

Stone, Julie, 1970-
 Try, try again / Julie Stone.
  p. cm.
 ISBN 978-0-8034-7724-7 (acid-free paper) 1. Single
mothers—Fiction. 2. Life change events—Fiction.
3. Divorce—Fiction. 4. Parents' and teachers'
associations—Fiction. 5. Widowers—Fiction.
I. Title.
PS3619.T6568T79 2011
813'.6—dc22

                                        2010037156

PRINTED IN THE UNITED STATES OF AMERICA
ON ACID-FREE PAPER
BY RR DONNELLEY, BLOOMSBURG, PENNSYLVANIA

This book is dedicated to moms of every kind:
working, stay-at-home, and everyone in between.
To the network of moms who keep me sane, Nancy,
Kelley, Kathy, Ann, Connie, Brooke, Janet, and Kristi.
To my mom, Mary. To the delightful boys
who call me Mom, Jake and Brett. And to Chad,
without whom nothing good in my life
would be possible.

Acknowledgments

Thanks, as always, to the great group of woman in my critique group. Shelley Shepard Gray, Heather Webber, Cathy Liggett, and Hilda Lindner Knepp. As Wilbur said about Charlotte, "It isn't often that someone comes along who is a true friend and a good writer." You ladies are both. Thank you for all your love, support, and help over the past seven years. I miss you all.

Chapter One

You're sure this is how we do it?" Riley Andrews looked around her usually impeccable kitchen and wondered for the hundredth time just how in the world it had come to this.

Riley was an advertising executive. She could command the attention of millions with just one catchy jingle. People jumped at the chance to come to one of her brainstorming meetings. She had her finger directly on the pulse of her target demographic—women ages 20 to 35. Or she *had*—past tense. Five months ago she had been all those things. Today, she was learning to make frosting from her eight-year-old son.

It wasn't making the frosting that bothered her, and it certainly, without a doubt, wasn't spending time with Noah. Any precious seconds she got with him were like snow on Christmas morning to her. Simply put, it was that she didn't know what she was doing. And being clueless about something, even something as simple as frosting, was the one thing in the world Riley couldn't stand.

1

And there had been a lot of it going around in the last five months.

"I'm sure. You have to make a paste out of the butter and sugar before you add the milk." He was adamant, and so she listened.

Two sticks of butter—check.

Two cups of powdered sugar—check.

One teaspoon vanilla—check.

She let Noah cream them together with a fork, watching as a line of intensity formed across his forehead. He turned the bowl slowly as he did it, making sure no speck of sugar was left. She admired his attention to detail.

That, most definitely, came from her side of his gene pool.

He looked up and gave her a broad smile. Happiness shone in his hazel eyes. They had the same gold flecks as hers, and his delight calmed her like an elixir. Noah's adjustment to this new living situation was all that mattered to Riley. Any thoughts of male companionship stopped and started with the blond-haired boy sitting across the counter from her. Period.

"All right, we're ready for the milk!" he announced, setting the bowl in front of her.

"You are going to pour," she said, picking up the hand mixer in her right hand while handing him the cup of milk with her left. "And I am going to do the beating."

"I want to do the beating," he said, not in a whiny voice, but in more of a "you can't get what you don't ask for" way. Another trait Riley knew he had inherited from her.

So she handed him the mixer, which he turned on and sunk into the creamy paste. Riley suddenly felt a wave of excitement about making the frosting with her son. It was the most domestic thing she had done in months, years, maybe her entire life. With great fanfare, she poured the milk into the bowl.

What happened next, she didn't anticipate. Pouring the milk while the mixer blades were whirling created automatic-weapon fire; the liquid shot out of the bowl and splattered everywhere.

"Turn it off! Turn it off!" she shrieked.

Noah, not knowing any better, lifted the mixer out of the bowl, confusion on his eight-year-old face. He was unsure just what had gone wrong—and continued to go wrong. The still-whirling blades sprayed Riley in the face, covering her with a substance that was nowhere near frosting.

She grabbed the mixer out of his hand and flipped the switch that turned it off, blinking as the sticky substance dripped from her bangs and into her eyes.

"That's not what happens when Dad does it." Noah's voice betrayed the bewilderment of a child who thought he knew how to do something he didn't.

Riley sighed. Her domestic-goddess moment had disappeared in the flick of the switch of a hand mixer. She looked around the kitchen. The counter and all the cupboards were covered in milk that was just sticky enough from the powdered sugar to make a real mess. Bending over, she caught sight of herself in the toaster. The dripping frosting highlighted her brown hair. But across the counter from her Noah was giggling. As it always did, that giggle made her smile.

Who cared if there was the mess to deal with? And who cared that they still didn't have any frosting for the two dozen cupcakes that were "required" for the welcome-back-to-school party the PTA was throwing?

The "corporate" Riley did, but she was quickly learning that the "hands-on mom" just couldn't. As many times as she'd thought to herself that managing the junior ad executives was like dealing with children, she'd been dead wrong. This was much better.

"How about we just use the stuff in the can?" she asked, pulling paper towels off the roll and winding them around her hand.

"Dad says that stuff tastes like glue," Noah replied, in a voice that sounded so like his father's she froze.

It was well and good for his father to have such a strong opinion about frosting, but he wasn't here to make it, not anymore.

Daniel had become "frustrated by their household arrangement." He'd said so out of the clear blue one Thursday. It didn't seem to matter that the "arrangement" had been his idea, something he'd come up with when she'd gotten pregnant and he was between jobs, as he had been so often in their ten-year marriage.

"You're on your way up the ladder, no stopping you, and I just haven't found my calling yet," he'd said, his hand rubbing her still-flat stomach in a way that, at the time, she had found so endearing. "Maybe a stay-at-home dad is what I'm supposed to be?"

It seemed the perfect solution. She'd had Noah, and then, after her maternity leave, returned to her job, leaving her baby in the comfort of his own home under the watchful eye of her surprisingly capable husband. Daniel knew exactly what to do when it came to taking care of their son, which was amazing to Riley, who couldn't discern one cry from the other.

And for eight years it had worked like clockwork. It seemed it truly was Daniel's calling. He'd thrived on the chaos that came along with staying home. The play dates and the mom-and-tot classes, where he was the only dad. He'd taken charge of all of it. He scheduled the pediatrician appointments and the dental exams. There wasn't one part of Noah's life that Daniel didn't take care of, and though at times Riley felt left out, she still marveled at the job he did. She knew she wouldn't have been nearly as good at all of it as he was.

That was why it had been so shocking when Daniel had made his announcement, packed his bags, and abandoned both of them.

Well, really just her.

He called Noah pretty regularly, though he'd not seen the boy since he moved out. He'd rented a loft apartment in the city, not that far away. To discover himself, he'd told her.

Riley couldn't wait until he discovered what it was like to have to pay his own bills for a change. That would bring him running back. And though, at the moment, she wished he would appear and make the dang frosting, generally, the vision of Daniel begging her to take him back ended with her slamming the door in his face.

It had been rough, but she and Noah were finding their way. The truth was that she was enjoying being the one to take care of her son. It filled a void in her she hadn't even known was there. And it was going well, up until she got the e-mail from the PTA, another gift from Daniel that kept on giving.

In the time she'd been on 100 percent mom duty, she had received 242 e-mails from the PTA and the various subcommittees Daniel had joined. It was more than she received in her day job, the one that paid the bills. The one she had taken a leave of absence from until she could figure out what a life without a stay-at-home dad would be like. Until she made sure that Noah was all right.

This brought her back to the cupcakes and the making of them even though she had no idea how to bake or frost.

Obviously.

"And in this case, glue isn't good?" she asked, recalling a boy in her third-grade class who had popped the top off many a bottle of Elmer's.

"Nope," Noah replied, running his finger through the soggy sugar and butter and licking it.

"Well, then, let's clean this up and try again." She handed him the wad of paper towels.

"If at first you don't succeed, try, try again," Noah said, grabbing the towels and shooting her a big grin.

Riley smiled back, and not just for his determination. "Try, try again" was one of her favorite sayings. Somehow, Noah saying it made her feel like maybe she wasn't so bad at this mothering thing after all.

Chapter Two

Riley had never felt so out of place in all her life. She glanced around the cafeteria at the other women, in their capri pants with coordinating tops, and tried to pretend she wasn't wearing a power suit. In her mind it had been the obvious choice for an introductory meeting, but, as was so often the case in her new life, she was wrong.

In her career, she'd grown used to being the only woman in a room full of men. Being the minority was something she had thrived on her entire professional life, a tactic she used, actually, to get the competitor off his game. But this situation was a whole new ball game. She was in the majority sexwise, but in the minority as far as the culture was concerned. She didn't know a thing about the PTA, only that her being a part of it was important for Noah.

The room was crammed full, and the level of chitchat was enough to make a sane person's ears ring. And interestingly, not only did their outfits match—the women themselves seemed to look remarkably similar. Their hair was perfectly highlighted, cut either fashionably short or held back in a tight ponytail. They were all wearing makeup, although not in a way that was obvious, but Riley knew no one's skin looked that perfect. She wondered if any of her campaigns had convinced them to buy the age-defying creams that they smeared on their faces every night.

They all wore minimal jewelry, Riley noted as she inched her way through the masses, except for the enormous diamond rings planted on each of their left hands. Self-consciously, she glanced down at the bare spot on her own hand where a similar ring had once sat, and she clenched her fingers together.

She wondered why Daniel had never poked fun at this whole scene to her. But then, she realized, maybe he hadn't seen the joke.

The last e-mail, the one explaining exactly where and when she was supposed to bring the cupcakes that the previous e-mail had told her to bake, had in no way prepared her for the atmosphere she had entered. All the correspondence had been overly bright and friendly, typed in a curlicue font and punctuated with plenty of those annoying smiley faces. She had imagined the PTA to be welcoming. That the women would be her refuge, helping her as she navigated these uncharted waters that her soon-to-be ex-husband had sailed for the past three years.

She couldn't have been more wrong.

These women were like lionesses on the savanna. They strutted around, protecting their turf from the outsider, the one so ignorant that she dared to show up in *professional attire*. A fatal error from which Riley knew she might never recover the moment she walked into the place.

"Can I help you?"

It was not a greeting, more like an order—as in, "Can I help remove you from this place where I reign and you do not fit in?"

"I'm Riley Andrews, Noah's mom," Riley stammered, trying hard to adjust once again to feeling like she didn't know what she was supposed to be doing.

Her mind scrambled, searching for something that would make her a part of this pack, or at the very least make her not stick out quite so much.

"I brought my cupcakes!" She said that last bit too loudly, too brightly, as she seized upon it—she had done as instructed. She had made cupcakes.

"Noah's *mom*?" the woman replied, ignoring the cupcakes. "Well, this is a first. Is Daniel ill?"

"Daniel has decided to reassess his priorities," Riley said tightly, hoping that this bit of information would grant her just a bit of sympathy. "So you get me this year." She hoped it sounded more like a gift than a booby prize, but she could tell from the look on the woman's face that she considered Riley far from a gift.

"Lucky us," the woman quipped, not a hint of welcome in her voice. "It is nice that you've decided to do the same." She smiled, but not sweetly.

"The same?" Riley asked, not sure what the woman was talking about.

"Reassess your priorities." Now the smile reeked of satisfaction. "All the same, we will miss Daniel. He was a tremendous asset to the group."

And without a word as to where Riley could put her cupcakes, the woman turned on her heel, swallowed up by the group of ponytailed, same-faced women who seemed to all know exactly what they were supposed to be doing.

In comfortable surroundings, Riley would have strode to the front of the room, commanded the attention of this group, and found out just where in the heck she was supposed to put her stupid cupcakes. Who knew that pastries would become such an obstacle? But she was completely out of her element and smart enough to know that one more wrong step and there would be no way to fix things. For Noah's sake, she needed to fit in. She slinked to the rows of folding chairs in the back of the room and sat down, holding onto her Tupperware and hoping she would be able to figure it out on her own.

"The food goes on the table at the front, according to category." The whispered voice came from behind her, so close she could feel the person's breath on her neck. Its decidedly male tone took Riley by surprise.

She turned and was equally shocked by the disarmingly deep blue eyes that greeted her.

"Category?" she stammered.

He stood and squeezed between the chairs to sit down next to her. "You know—fruit, crackers, muffins—*category.*" He smiled, small lines forming around those eyes. He was a very handsome man; in addition to the eyes, there were the brown hair, cut short, a square jaw, and cheekbones. He looked like the cover of that *Men's Health* magazine Daniel used to read.

Daniel.

Even if he was a jerk, she was still married to him.

Focus on the PTA.

Looking through the clear top of the container on her lap, the man snapped his fingers and pointed.

"Ah, cupcakes."

She followed his gesture to the end of the folding table at the front of the room, the one that sat under a banner that read HUBBARD SCHOOL PTA WELCOMES YOU BACK.

It was an obvious location. Heat flooded her cheeks, and she stood quickly and crossed the room, depositing the cupcakes that she and Noah had been so proud of but now looked a little on the pathetic side. Retracing her steps back to her chair, it was hard to ignore the whispers that trailed behind her as she passed, but she kept her eyes forward.

"Thanks," she said, sitting back down. "You're the first helpful person I've met today."

He nodded, smiling knowingly, and Riley felt that

she had found an ally. "You're new, then. Just moved to town?"

Riley shook her head. "My soon-to-be ex-husband was the PTA guy. So this is all new to me."

She hoped she didn't sound as bitter as she felt whenever she said that whole "soon-to-be-ex" thing. It was so expected that she would be bitter, and she didn't want to be a stereotype.

"Oh, I'm sorry to hear that" was all he said, though the sympathy on his face put her at ease. She smiled slightly.

"According to the litany of e-mails I've been getting from this group, I'm supposed to find some woman named Sam Aldin to change all of my contact information and get my orientation materials." She laughed to herself at the absurdity of such a simple thing having to be so formal.

The PTA took itself very seriously.

"Which one of these overly chipper harpies do you think she is?" she asked before she could stop herself.

He was here, after all; she couldn't exclude him from the PTA stereotype simply because of his gender.

"How do you know she's one of them?" he asked, leaning in close enough for Riley to notice that he smelled delicious. And twice in as many minutes she felt calmed by his voice.

"Please, a name like Sam?" She rolled her eyes. "Women with cute nicknames at this age are not only one of them, they are generally the ringleaders."

He laughed again, and against her better judgment, not to mention her newly formed distrust of men, she found that she liked making this handsome man laugh.

Stealing a sideways glance, she was reassured by something else—the gold band on the third finger of his left hand. She didn't have to hate married men, those willing to stand by their commitments.

The sound of a whistle halted their conversation and a silence filled the room. The women quickly scurried to find seats. All but one, that is. A tall woman, her blond hair cascading in waves as perfect as in any shampoo commercial Riley'd ever written a jingle for, her blue eyes twinkling as brightly as the diamonds in her ears, stood at the front of the room.

"Welcome back to school, all you PTA'ers!" she said in a honey-toned voice that made the hair on the back of Riley's neck stand up.

But that was nothing compared to the response.

The room as a whole erupted in cheers and whistles. The seemingly reserved women stomped their feet and clapped their hands in unison with abandon. Riley turned to her newfound ally, her mouth agape, her eyes wide.

"What in the world?" she whispered, leaning into him so she could be heard above all the hoopla.

"The kids going back to school means they are off duty," he whispered.

Riley was appalled. These women, who she had always felt judged by for her choice to have a career, were celebrating the start of school so they could be rid of their kids? She glanced around the room at their ecstatic faces, unbelieving.

"Ironic, isn't it?" He sighed, sitting back in his chair and crossing his foot over his knee.

"That wasn't the adjective I was thinking of, actually," she replied, feeling the years of judgment fall off her, replaced by sheer irritation.

A swarm of shushing soon quieted the cheering, and Blondie commanded the room once again.

"I'm sure it will be another productive and fun year for the entire family here at Hubbard Elementary School." Her eyes widened as she spoke, and her hands waved in front of her.

"She looks just like a Sam, doesn't she? Sam Aldin, Sammy, Samantha." The man beside her smiled knowingly.

"I won't keep you from the treats with a long speech," she continued. "Our first business meeting is next Tuesday morning. But please make use of the sign-up sheets by the door so we can hit the ground running."

The women all pulled out their calendars and scribbled furiously, as if missing the business meeting would be the end-all of their lives. Riley refused to write it down, instead committing it to memory and taking note that her new ally didn't write it down either.

"Remember the cupcakes at the end are for the kids."

Again they all nodded their heads in unison.

"For now, let's just all enjoy the celebration!"

Cue the raucous cheering, and Riley once again rolled her eyes.

"I love my son, but I don't know if I can do this on a regular basis," she said, shaking her head.

"You figure out how to tune it out," he said calmly, not seeming to notice the women thundering past him to the table filled with food.

"I'd better go find this Sam," Riley said, peering around the room wanting to make a run for it much more than to actually sign up for this group. "I'm sure she will be completely thrilled to meet me."

"Yeah, that suit is a dead giveaway."

Riley laughed. Maybe it wouldn't be so bad, if he came to all the meetings. He was at the very least sane, even if she had to ignore how handsome he was.

She held out her hand. "I'm Riley Andrews."

"Sam Aldin," he said, the smile on his face never changing, as Riley felt the familiar sense of mortification creeping through her entire body.

Chapter Three

Sam tried hard to stay focused on the conversation he was having with Megan Yearly, but his eyes kept darting around the room hoping to catch a glimpse of Riley. His not-so-smooth introduction had embarrassed her. He knew he probably should have told her sooner, but, in his defense, she hadn't given him much of a chance.

He regretted it now, as her embarrassment had caused her to flee to the other side of the room and left him stuck talking to Megan. Karma, he supposed.

Megan was going on and on about the school supply sale, and did he think it was a better fundraiser than wrapping paper? Sam didn't actually have an opinion. He hadn't seen the numbers, but that was beside the point. At his son's last school, where being the only man on the PTA had been equally as novel, he'd learned to do a great deal of nodding during the general discussions.

He'd heard rumors that there was another active father in this PTA. The idea that he would have another male, a dad as dedicated as he was, had thrilled him.

But it was safe to assume he was Riley's soon-to-be ex. So, once again Sam would be the only father. After a small sample of Riley's biting humor, however, he thought it might be a fair trade.

It wouldn't take long, Sam knew, before the whole group learned his story. He was a widower with an eight-year-old son. His wife had died of breast cancer three years earlier. He'd moved to this small town, close enough to Chicago to be considered a suburb though it was a hefty commute, to give his son the sense of community Sam himself had experienced as a child.

What they wouldn't learn, with their sympathetic looks and offers to cook dinner or babysit Max, was that though Sam had made peace with his wife's death, he would never truly be over her. Maggie had been the love of his life, and he didn't see that changing anytime soon. He'd made peace with that too. Max was his focus—their son and the spitting image of his mother. He was the most important thing in Sam's world.

Subconsciously, he knew that was probably one of the reasons he immersed himself in this group of married women. The pack of them had never failed to make him want to spend more time with his son and very little time with the opposite sex. But that was before Riley sat down in front of him, looking as displaced as he felt most of the time. A female friend wasn't out of the question. And from the look of her, she could use the help.

"It sounds like there are some solid opportunities for fundraising," he said, hoping to put an end to the conversation. He smiled slightly at Megan. "Now, if you'll excuse me, I need to go and collect the information on our other new members."

Megan made a face, the kind Max used to make when, as a baby, he'd been fed strained peas.

"I'm sure Ms. Business Suit will be pleased to give you her number."

When Sam didn't reply, she continued.

"It was so nice talking to you, Sam. Welcome to the Hubbard PTA." It was a rote response, one he had heard when he contacted the president and the membership director. Sam had volunteered to keep the database of members, mostly because it gave him an out—it was a role that didn't require his presence all the time.

"I hope I get to meet your wife, really soon."

Instinctively, he twisted the gold wedding band he still wore on his ring finger.

"Nice talking to you," he said.

There was no easy response to that statement, and they would all know soon enough. Until they did, it was nice to not have to deal with their sad looks of sympathy. That was another reason he had decided to relocate—to get away from the well-intended, but never-ending, sympathy.

Now, as he made his way through the crowd toward the food table, he was careful not to make eye contact with any of them, not wanting to get caught up in another conversation about fundraising or whatever. So far, this PTA was vastly different from the organization at Max's last school. That one had been made up of overly eager mothers as well, but they hadn't seemed quite so much like a sorority. In this group, it seemed, being made to feel like you had to earn your place was par for the course. He agreed with Riley, he loved his son, but this assemblage might just be asking a bit much of his patience.

The spread on the banquet table was impressive, not just prebought goodies and veggie trays, but homemade cookies and muffins, and even the vegetables looked hand cut. Sam helped himself to a plate and filled it. He could cook, but baking wasn't something he had mastered. Thank goodness for bake-and-break cookies, or he'd have nothing even remotely homemade.

"Psst."

The sound was coming from around the corner, behind the folding accordion doors that so regularly graced elementary schools, the kind they use to divide rooms when there are too many children and too much noise for the grown-ups in charge to manage.

"Sam, over here." There was urgency in the whisper, and so he followed it, intrigued. The door was open just a crack, and as he leaned forward to peer inside, a hand reached out from the darkened room and pulled him inside.

"What the . . . ," he stammered, not sure what had happened, just that whoever had yanked on his arm was strong. Freakishly strong.

"Sorry about that," the familiar voice muttered. As

his eyes adjusted to the darkness, he wasn't all that surprised to see who it was.

"Riley," he said, chuckling softly.

"I know, I know. But I decided my embarrassing moment with you was less painful than the firing squad out there." She stepped closer to him, and he could see her eyes were wide and wild, as though they were somehow being held hostage.

"How are we going to get out of here?"

"The door?" he suggested, enjoying her panic probably just a little too much.

"Very funny. You aren't the one who's getting it stuck to them. Those women have an opinion about everything! From my choice of clothing to the fact that prior to this I held a full-time job, not to mention my haircut." Her hands came to rest on her hips. "And they are happy to tell me that that is exactly why my husband walked out on me."

Her whisper was fierce and fast. From experience, Sam knew what it was like to have a room full of people passing judgment on you that they had no business making. He'd felt sorry for her earlier, standing there with her Tupperware full of melting cupcakes, but now what he felt was more like a kinship.

He peered out the crack of the door, searching for something that could distract the masses. His eyes seized on a silver platter piled high with chocolate cookies. It was sitting perilously close to the edge of the table and on the opposite corner from the door.

"All right. I'll distract them, and you can make a run for it. But I have one condition," he whispered over his shoulder.

"Anything."

This whole experience was wrought with more drama than the espionage movie he'd rented last week. And it was more than a little exciting, since he was playing the hero in this PTA version.

"I don't want them all over me for not doing my job, so I need your contact information." He said it with as much tension as he could muster, copying the very spy he'd watched in the movie.

A smile broke out across her face, and Riley reached into her pocket and handed him her business card.

"Okay," he said, shoving it into his pocket. "Here goes, and if I don't make it out of here in one piece, try to go on without me."

He winked at her still-smiling face and started toward the door. He paused, looked both ways, then slipped out without being seen.

Walking quickly through the door, he made his way to the tray and, after grabbing a handful of cookies, flipped it off the table, sending it clattering to the linoleum floor.

Throngs of women descended on him, picking the cookies off the floor and patting his arm in an attempt, he was sure, to reassure him that they didn't blame him for his offense. It did cross his mind that if Riley had done this exact same thing, they would have strung her

up by the heels of her designer pumps. He feigned re-
morse.

"I don't know how I managed to do that," he exclaimed, shrugging as they fussed over him. Though he
didn't enjoy being mothered, he allowed it, because it
was for a good cause.

The last thing Sam saw of Riley was her disappear-
ing through the door to the hall. She paused briefly to
look back through the window and shoot him a smile
that made all the commotion worthwhile.

Chapter Four

*S*urely *this is what being thrown into the lion's den in Roman times felt like,* Riley thought as she pulled into the drop-off line in front of Noah's school. Or, more accurately, how it felt to run a gauntlet, with people lined up on both sides to take a whack at you.

It was a picturesque gauntlet. A long, curving road lined with neatly trimmed hedges leading to a redbrick building, it was the perfect suburban elementary school. Complete with a WELCOME BACK TO SCHOOL banner that hung over the entrance. Everything was as it should be, orderly and welcoming. Only Riley was out of place.

Even her car was wrong. The sleek black sedan she adored stuck out like a sore thumb in the sea of minivans and giant SUVs surrounding her. It didn't matter in the least that hers was more practical and fuel efficient; it was just another reminder to the women who surrounded her, and to herself, that she was different.

Riley took a deep breath and tried to regain her composure. It was Noah's first day of third grade—this was supposed to be about him, not about the crazies who had bombarded her with e-mails and phone messages about committees and meetings, and tried to "just confirm," one last time, that her husband really wasn't joining the PTA this year.

It was about Noah's new backpack and school supplies, about his choice to buy his lunch for the first week instead of pack. A blessing for which Riley thanked her lucky stars, as it bought her some time to figure out just what she was supposed to pack. Breakfast had gone smoothly. Noah had always been more partial to frozen waffles than homemade.

And now here they were. Noah—dressed in his special first-day-of-school outfit of a short-sleeved, plaid shirt and new shorts, and, most important, new sneakers—inching ever closer to the building. For the first time, Riley felt something close to gratitude toward Daniel for leaving. After all, if he were here, she wouldn't be participating in this ritual. The grateful feeling was strange. She had spent the better part of the last few months seething at the mere mention of his name.

"How're you doing back there, buddy?" she asked, catching her son's eye in the rearview mirror. He had heard from his friend Timmy that his teacher might be a bit of a yeller. And Riley had confirmed it the night before with Amanda Stiles, the class mom who had called to introduce herself.

"I'm sure its going to be fine, sweetheart," Riley told Noah, hoping it was the truth. "Maybe last year was just a bad one for Mrs. Vicks?"

"Do you think so, really?" Noah asked, his voice sounding small and unsure.

"Yes, I do," she said, trying to be more assured herself, though the guilt of confirming his fear filled her.

"Think about it, buddy, all those moms from school who called, and only Mrs. Stiles said your teacher was a yeller."

"Maybe Mrs. Stiles did something wrong?" Noah asked.

No, Mommy did. Another lesson learned: never, ever pass along inside teacher information to your child.

The gratitude that she had been feeling just moments earlier evaporated with the quiver in her son's voice, and Riley cursed her husband for leaving her to navigate all these rules on her own.

Riley inched her car forward behind an enormous black SUV, her eyes even with its bumper.

"You did get an awful lot of calls about school." His voice sounded more relaxed, more like himself, and Riley felt a bit of her guilt subside.

"Mm-hmm," she muttered, distracted by the decree on the bumper sticker in front of her that proclaimed the driver's love for her dog.

It boggled Riley's mind that someone would go to the trouble of putting a sticker on their car for something as inane as dog love.

"I've never heard the phone ring so much."

That was an understatement. Since she had taken on the full-time-mom role, and suddenly the PTA role, her phone rang nonstop.

The only person she hadn't heard from was Sam. She found his lack of contact frustrating, and then she was equally as irritated at herself for caring. She tried to reason that it was simply because he had been the only rational person at the PTA party. That she would have been equally offended if Sam was a woman who had blown her off. But try as she might to be reasonable, she still felt let down every time the phone rang and the caller ID didn't say Sam Aldin.

The beep of a horn snapped her out of her fog. The sound was not a friendly tap. This was a loud, full, hand-on-the-horn blast that made Riley slam on her brakes and grab the wheel with both hands as she jumped. When it stopped, and when she realized she was not about to be broadsided by a semi or rear-ended by an out-of-control school bus, Riley slammed her car into park and jumped out.

From the expression on the honking woman's face, it was clear it wasn't an accidental honking. No, the woman meant business, but, as irritated as she was, so did Riley.

She marched back toward the minivan behind her only to discover the window of the driver's door still rolled up and the woman, a small blond, perfectly made up and wearing a tennis outfit, miming confusion.

Riley, trying to ignore the fact that she was dressed in sweats, as she hadn't been organized enough to shower, let alone put regular clothes on, tapped on the glass. The woman rolled the window down just far enough so she could speak. "You are holding up the line!" She pointed a perfectly manicured finger straight at Riley, in case there was a doubt just who she was accusing.

Riley drew in a deep breath and attempted to gather herself before speaking. "I realize that, but a polite reminder tap of the horn would have sufficed."

Nicely done. I said my piece and didn't even throttle the woman.

Riley smiled at the accomplishment. But within seconds, her tightly stretched patience was once again put to the test.

"I mean, *now*. You are holding up the line *now*!"

If Riley hadn't been so irritated to begin with, the small blond woman's perfect imitation of a petulant two-year-old would have been laugh-out-loud funny. As it was, however, it was the proverbial straw that broke the camel's back.

"Listen lady, all I'm saying is that you didn't have to lay on the horn . . ."

The woman waved her hand in the air and then pinched her fingers together in a gesture Riley had seen in a movie once. She was telling Riley to close her mouth.

"You are obviously new to the drop-off. We have procedures to follow in the car line. You never put your car in park. Keep your eye on the bumper in front of you. Your child should be seated on the passenger side." She leaned around to look at the back of the sedan, where Noah's head could clearly be seen behind the driver's seat.

"Looks like someone didn't read their procedure manual," she scolded, cocking her head to one side.

"Now if you could please get back in your car and keep the line moving. I'm going to be late for my tennis match."

Riley opened her mouth to tell the woman just where exactly she could put her procedure manual, but her voice was drowned out by the blare of a car horn. The small blond woman, her hand pressing firmly on the horn, rolled the window up, and stared at Riley with fire in her eyes.

Dumbstruck and completely enraged by the way she had been dismissed, Riley put her hands on her hips, refusing to budge. Then, suddenly, the one horn was joined by another, and then another, until all the cars in the line were pounding on their horns. The noise was deafening, and Riley's mouth fell open. But it wasn't until their perfectly coiffed heads started poking out the windows of their enormous automobiles that she turned on her heel and walked slowly back to her car.

"Why is everyone honking?" Noah asked, turning to look out the back window,

"Everyone's just really happy about the first day of school," Riley said too brightly. "Now slide over to the other side of the car, sweets. We wouldn't want to slow down the car line."

Riley put her car in drive and inched forward, her mind spinning. This was much worse than she had imagined. It was like visiting a foreign country, and not only could she not speak the language, she couldn't even gesture to get her point across.

If only she had an interpreter.

Her foot slipped off the gas as the realization hit her. She did have an interpreter, and not just any old run-of-the-mill one, at that. She bit her tongue to keep from screaming out in pure joy. It was a sign of her stress level that it had taken her so long to figure out she had exactly what she needed all along.

Riley might not know much about school politics, but she was smart enough to know when she needed help. And as she reached the front of the line and dropped her son off for his first day of school, she picked up the cell phone sitting on the front seat and dialed her own personal version of the cavalry.

"Tricia Livingston!" the bright bubbly voice at the other end of the phone chirped.

"Trish, I need your help," Riley said, hoping she sounded more sincere than desperate.

"Why, Riley, in my whole life, I never thought I'd hear those words from my big sister!"

Riley cringed at the reply, because she agreed wholeheartedly. She'd never needed help from the sister who was her polar opposite. But desperate times called for desperate measures.

"Neither did I, but if there is one thing I'm good at, it's calling in the experts, and in this case that is you," she replied.

"And just what, in your opinion, am I such an expert at?" Her sister's tone was not mocking, but truly intrigued.

"The Hubbard School PTA."

"Tomorrow, nine A.M., Coffee Chic." Tricia answered without missing a beat. "Gotta run!"

And the line went dead. In another lifetime, the reply would have seemed to Riley to be both condescending and overly dramatic, but now the only thing she felt was relief. That, and a hint of optimism. Perhaps she was on the way to solving her problem. There was hope.

Chapter Five

It was a tradition they had started as a family on Max's first day of preschool: ice cream and a trip to the park. The first time they'd done it without Maggie, it had been tearful. But three years later, it wasn't nearly as melancholy, and Sam had found himself looking forward to it more and more as the clock inched ever closer to three.

Only the ice cream flavors changed. Max was digging into a big bowl of cake batter, which tasted remarkably like its namesake, without, Sam assumed, the raw eggs. He, on the other hand, was working on a waffle cone full to the top with peanut butter fudge.

They were sitting on a bench near the dog run, the sun low enough that the shadows of the trees reached the tip of the path though the air still clung to the afternoon heat. So far, Max had been silent about his first day as he dug in the bowl of ice cream for the pieces of brownie he had added.

"So, it sounds like you had a pretty good day, overall," Sam said, trying to pull a bit more information out of his son. He had learned over the years that it took a few tries to get the boy to open up about the time he spent at school.

"Yeah, I like Mrs. Swish, and our room is cool. She likes fish, so the whole thing looks like it's underwater," Max answered, ice cream dripping off his chin. "And she has an awesome aquarium."

"It does sound cool," Sam answered, taking a bite of his own cone and feeling a tug at his heart for his son's enthusiasm over something like the set-up of his classroom. He thought about leaning across and wiping Max's chin, but then thought better of it. Instead, he handed Max a napkin, which he crumpled into a ball, neglecting to wipe his face.

There were moments when Sam missed his late wife: her company, her point of view, or her sense of humor. But then there were times like this, when, instead, he felt so sorry that she wasn't able to experience something as simple and pure as their son's description of his third-grade classroom.

It was a beautiful afternoon. The sun was warm enough to make the ice cream a treat, but the breeze hinted at the coming change of season. Big, billowing clouds seemed to be racing across the patches of clear blue sky visible between the trees.

"That one looks like a turtle," Max said, pointing with his spoon at a cloud that hung low.

"It does," Sam replied, and then his eyes scanned the

heavens, looking at each of the clouds until he, too, saw something in them.

"That one looks like an owl." He pointed to one higher up.

Beside him, Max tilted his head back and tried to follow his father's finger, but Sam could tell by the look on his face that he didn't know which cloud Sam was pointing out.

He put his arm around his son's shoulders and held his hand up in Max's line of vision. "That one, up above the skinny one, see it? It's long, with a point at the bottom?"

"Where?" Max tilted his head and squinted, his gaze staying even with Sam's finger, his eyes searching but not finding the cloud.

"Do you see the turtle?"

Max nodded.

"Then follow my finger up from there." Sam drew a line across the span of blue from one cloud to the other, and he could tell from the jolt in Max's shoulders when he made the connection. They sat in silence enjoying their small cloud zoo, each doing his best to finish what remained of his ice cream.

"Look at that puppy!" Max exclaimed a few minutes later, ending the peace of the moment.

"Which one?" Sam asked, his eyes skimming the skyline.

"Not a cloud one, Dad, a real one!" Max was pointing excitedly toward the entrance to the dog run, where there was, in fact, a real live puppy. But it wasn't the dog that caught Sam's attention, it was the woman who held tightly to the leash.

Riley Andrews.

Since their initial meeting less than a week earlier, Sam had often thought about the flustered woman who had seemed more out of place than he had at the PTA meeting. He'd even picked up his phone to call her on more than one occasion, but he had never completed the task.

He tried to tell himself that he wasn't calling her because he didn't really have anything to say to her. But the truth was that he wasn't calling her because of the way he had so blatantly asked for her number. He had been so drawn to her, so distracted by her mere presence at the meeting. It was troubling to him.

Sam still considered himself married, and asking Riley for her number seemed like infidelity. It wasn't as though he hadn't gotten phone numbers from other women, but not in a way that was so personal, so flirtatious. So not-the-man-he-was at this stage in his life, and the departure from his normal way of being was startling.

And now, here she was, standing across the park, looking completely composed and holding the leash of the rather tiny puppy his son was running to meet.

Sam collected himself, and the empty ice cream bowl, and followed, though not at Max's breakneck pace.

Again, the mere sight of Riley caused him to smile, and a feeling of excitement coursed through him. Both were met with an attempt to squelch them. He would have much rather regained his composure before greeting her, but with Max descending on her puppy and a boy he assumed was her son, he couldn't very well do that.

By the time he joined them, Max was just about to throw his arms around the puppy when Riley stopped him.

"You need to let him smell your hand first," she said gently. "He's just a baby, and he might nip if you don't let him get a whiff of you."

She smiled down at Max, with no trace of the stress or bewilderment that had been plastered on her face the last time Sam had seen her.

Max held his hand out to the puppy. The sweet thing pushed his long nose into the open palm, audibly sniffing at it before finally giving Max his seal of approval with a swipe of his tongue. That was followed by a wag of his tail that soon overtook his whole body until his entire frame was shimmying from side to side.

Max erupted into giggles, and so did the boy who stood with Riley.

"Isn't he great? His name's Ralph. We just got him today!" the boy exclaimed.

Max nodded, unable to answer, as the puppy had moved on from his hand to the remnants of ice cream that were around his mouth.

Riley let out a laugh of her own, a sound as pure as

the two boys beside her. And despite his best effort to quash it, the smile on Sam's face spread as Riley glanced up and a look of recognition crossed her face.

"Sam Aldin, how nice it is to see you in a more pleasant setting." Her laughter had trailed off, but the smile on his face stayed.

Sam glanced around. In addition to the peals of laughter from the two boys and the excessive licking and tail wagging of the puppy, just inside the fence there were close to twenty other dogs running and barking. That, combined with the screams of delight coming from the playground down the path and the soccer game going on across the dog park, made the scene one of organized chaos. It was definitely more pleasant.

"My thoughts exactly," he said, and before he could stop himself, he winked.

Instantly flooded with embarrassment, he spoke quickly, hoping to recover some normalcy in the exchange. "This is my son, Max."

Max stood, and as he always did, offered his hand to Riley, who took it and shook it with a gentle tug.

"Nice to meet you, Max. This is my son, Noah. He's in third grade." Noah waved shyly from beside his mother.

"Me too!" Max exclaimed and the boys eyed each other.

"You want to go play on the monkey bars?" Noah asked, and Max looked to Sam for his approval before nodding yes.

"Just be careful," Riley called as the instant friends ran off in the direction of the playground, leaving Sam alone with Riley.

"That is one cute puppy," Sam said, looking down at the dog that yipped after the boys, straining on its leash, trying to go after them. It was a caramel color, and it was at that gangly stage of puppyhood in which its feet were too big and its legs were too long, giving it the appearance of a small child wearing his father's loafers.

Riley gave the leash a gentle tug, and the puppy quit his struggle and lay down to chew on a stick it had overturned.

"Isn't he?" Her smile softened as she reached down and took the stick away, giving his floppy ears a scratch.

"Do you mind if we move a little closer to the playground?" he asked, craning his neck to get a better look at where Max and Noah had run off.

"That's what I was about to say," she said, pulling gently on the dog's leash. The three of them started down the path. "I wasn't so sure if that was being neurotic— you know, shadowing my third grader at the park."

"I'm the wrong person to ask. I always err on the side of being a bit overprotective."

"Given my lack of experience, I'll trust you on this," she said, laughing a bit at herself.

They reached the edge of the playground and sat down on a bench. Riley pulled a piece of rawhide from her purse and handed it down to the puppy, who immediately collapsed and began chewing on it.

"Don't take this the wrong way, but I didn't really see you as a puppy person the first time we met."

She raised her eyebrows. "What exactly qualifies one as a 'puppy person'?"

"I would think you would need to be very calm and rational to have a puppy. And not, let's say, someone who hides behind a room divider to plot her escape from a PTA meeting."

"I would say escaping that meeting shows just how rational I am," Riley said emphatically. "And, for the record, I am a puppy person, a dog person. But my soon-to-be ex was allergic, so we couldn't have one."

"So the ex is out, the dog is in?"

"It's a bit deeper than that. When I was growing up, my parents trained seeing-eye dogs, and I loved having all those puppies around. Then, today, I was driving home from dropping Noah off at school, which, for the record, went about as well as the PTA meeting." She paused and rolled her eyes, then she continued. "I heard a news story on the radio about a shelter that had been shut down due to lack of funding. They needed people to take in the animals, or they would have to be put down. Before I knew it, my car was turning in that direction, and the rest is history."

She tilted her head to the side, looking around him to where the boys were playing and then bringing her gaze back to him, a shy smile on her face.

Sam nodded, surprised that the woman he was sitting next to was the same frazzled person he had met just a week earlier. It didn't fit that she would have the patience to train a puppy, and the contradiction made her even more intriguing, much to his dismay.

"It seems very rational. I stand corrected," was all he could manage to reply.

"Speaking of rational," she said, turning and pulling one leg up under the other and resting her hand on her knee. "Since you were the only *normal* person I met at that insane meeting, I was a bit disappointed that you were the only one who didn't call me. Care to explain?"

Her eyes twinkled mischievously, and Sam's mind raced back to all those times he'd picked up the phone. He opened his mouth to say something, but found that he had no words.

In his own, rational mind, he could think of no explanation for not calling the ever-more-intriguing Riley Andrews.

Chapter Six

Sitting at the small table at the coffeehouse, Riley wrestled with the idea of just getting up and leaving. It was bad enough that she'd had to call her sister for help, but to be kept waiting for more than half an hour was just completely irritating. Not that it was much of a surprise—Tricia had always been on her own schedule.

She flipped through the newspaper that was spread on the table in front of her, stopping on the business page to take in the headlines, then flipping to the stock report to see how her portfolio was holding up. All ordinary things she did every day, though never in a place like this. Riley had rolled her eyes at just the name *Coffee Chic* when Tricia had suggested it.

With its dim lighting and mismatched furniture, they were obviously going for a thrift-store vibe. The whole thing was a bit over-the-top for Riley. If she wanted to be a part of this trendy scene, she wouldn't be living in the suburbs.

She checked her watch and took a sip of her straight

black coffee—no triple-vanilla-skim-with-foam any-thing for her.

It wasn't just the irritation at her sister's choice of meeting place that was making Riley antsy. It was her encounter in the park with Sam. Running into him had been a pleasant surprise. The conversation had been nothing earth-shattering; all Riley could focus on was the way he had looked at her—in the eye, never shifting his gaze as they carried on their seemingly benign con-versation. If only the boys hadn't descended on them right as she'd asked why he hadn't called, she might have gotten an answer.

Part of her really wanted to know. But the other part thanked her lucky stars for her son's small bladder. Their trip to the restroom had put an end to the im-promptu play date in the park. So the question remained unanswered. At the moment she was taking that in a "no news is good news" kind of way.

The bell on the door jingled a merry tune, and Riley looked up with the hope of seeing her sister, but the feeling was gone in a flash and instantly replaced by one of sheer horror.

It was not her sister who had arrived, but rather the women Riley had come to plot against.

An entire group of them, among them the woman from the car line, the cupcake coordinator at her first PTA meeting, and assorted other familiar, and implaca-ble, faces. They were all still wearing what Riley con-sidered their uniform: workout gear that looked as though a drop of sweat had never touched it. When Riley went for a run, she wore a pair of shorts and whatever T-shirt was on the top of the pile. She almost never matched, and it hadn't crossed her mind that she should.

With their sudden arrival, the forced quaintness of the coffeehouse became even more claustrophobic. Riley glanced around for an escape route, to no avail. They were between her and the door, so leaving was not an option. The route to the bathroom would take her right through the area where they were pulling chairs together like the cool kids in a grade-school lunchroom.

There seemed to be some sort of pecking order among the group. The cupcake lady and the one who'd made the speech at the first meeting sat down on the chairs that had been assembled for them by the carpool screamer and a woman Riley didn't know. Orders for coffee were taken by women who seemed overly anxious about getting the information right, like insecure freshmen at their first senior party.

As there was no way out, Riley grasped the edges of her newspaper, and she was about to shield herself with it when she was spotted by the carpool screamer, who was not-so-subtly pointing Riley out to a woman she had yet to meet. Riley waved meekly, fuming inside that this flock of women could so quickly reduce her to the timid oddball she had been in high school.

Oddball might be a bit strong. She hadn't worn a

pocket protector or had acne and a bad perm. She had been, however, more concerned with her grades than her date for Saturday night. And in her high school, that and a lack of knowledge of the Top 40 qualified her as an outsider.

There was no way she could hide behind her newspaper now that she had been spotted. Her hand grasped the edges of the paper, wadding it up in her fingers. She silently willed for her sister to appear so she could focus her irritation on an actual target. Staring blindly at the sports page, Riley found it impossible not to hear the loud whispering going on across the room.

Tales of her recent history were being thrown about like the storylines of a prime-time soap opera, in what she was sure they thought were hushed voices.

"Did you know her husband left her?"

"Probably because he was tired of doing everything!"

"I bet she never let him forget she was the one making the money."

"What is the deal with *her hair color*?"

They sounded like a bunch of chickens with laryngitis.

Riley was tempted to stand up and yell, "I can hear you, you know!"

But the jingle of the entrance bell stopped her, and a hush fell over the gathered crowd. Without even glancing over her shoulder, Riley knew from the change in the faces of the women across the room that her salvation had arrived. She set down the paper, folded her hands on the table in front of her, and waited for the show to begin.

"Oh. My. God."

The collective squeal burst from the group.

"Tricia Livingston!"

Prior to this newfound involvement with the PTA crowd, Riley had paid only partial attention to her sister's involvement in it. She had listened as well as she could as Trish described the work she was doing at the school—the meetings and the fundraisers, not to mention the gala. Her brainchild, she called it, as she had been the first to chair the event.

At the time, it seemed to Riley more than a little ridiculous. Her sister's calendar was more jam-packed than those of the CEOs of most corporations. She knew her sister was a big deal at school, but until this very moment, it hadn't been completely clear.

Trish hadn't just run the PTA: she *was* the PTA.

Up until two years ago, when her last child had moved on to the middle school and Trish had moved on herself. Now she organized fundraisers for various groups that needed her services. At the moment, though, no one needed her more than Riley did.

The faces of the women, who just moments earlier had looked refined and composed, were now flushed with excitement. They practically jumped up and down as Riley's sister made her entrance.

Hollywood stars on the red carpet and politicians working the crowd had nothing on her. She was dressed impeccably, in those trendy jeans with the big cuffs turned up and a short-sleeved cashmere sweater the exact color of her blue eyes. Her hair was a shiny, rich mahogany that only someone who knew her as a child would know was a dye job. She accessorized with tasteful, expensive jewelry, right down to the diamond ring on her left hand. It was smaller than those of the PTA crowd, but it was an heirloom from the Livingston family, so that gave it more stature than the giant rocks the rest of them wore.

They stared at her. The jaws of some of the women in the back of the crowd literally hung open, as though they were seeing the Queen of England or Bigfoot. It was hard to tell which. Both came with their own set of legends, and so did Tricia.

But instead of crossing the room to join her fans, Trish stopped beside Riley's table and let out a refined, but loud, greeting of her own.

"Riley! I am so sorry, how rude of me to keep my *sister* waiting!"

It was that last part that made Riley forgive Trish instantly for the protracted wait. The word seemed to hang in the air as one by one the faces of the women across the room crumpled into looks of confusion. Then, to add to their disillusionment, their idol pulled the intruder in their midst into a warm embrace.

Chapter Six

Listen up, I only have thirty minutes for this meeting, so we need to make the most of it." The urgency in Trish's voice did not match the broad smile on her face as she pulled out the chair next to Riley and sat down.

Riley, who was still basking in the effect of her sister's arrival, nodded.

"I was ready to wring your neck for making me sit here, amongst that gaggle, by myself. But your entrance, the looks on their faces, was well worth any pain and suffering. Do you want me to grab you a cup of coffee or something?" The thrill of this maneuver was like an adrenaline rush, and Riley's words spilled out with her enthusiasm.

Trish cut her off. "It's obvious that they have already marked you as an outsider. You're about one misstep away from being put in charge of book orders," she hissed, though the delighted expression on her face never changed. "We don't have time for mindless chatter or my coffee order."

Riley's eyes darted to the group across the room, their picture-perfect faces still filled with a mixture of shock and horror. She half expected the freshmen in the group to be dispatched for ice water to keep Cupcake and Screamer from fainting.

"Why is it so obvious? And why are book orders a bad thing?" Riley loved book orders; she pored over the ones that Noah brought home. And even though she knew she was a marked woman, it was intriguing that her sister could tell that in the twelve seconds that had ticked by since she arrived at the coffeehouse.

"Please. The way they've circled up over there— that is Hubbard PTA for 'there is an intruder in our midst.' Thank goodness you called me when you did." Trish turned and flashed a big smile at their audience and then wiggled her chair so that her back was now to them.

"See what I did there? Now they know without a doubt that we are on to them."

"Because you smiled at them?" Riley was confused.

"I smiled, and then I turned my back on them. It's a clear signal."

Trish said this as though every sane person in the world should know that. Like summer follows spring, or don't wear white after Labor Day.

A crushing sense of ineptness came over Riley. If she was expected to master such subtleties as smiling and chair turning, she was certain she'd never survive.

And, really, did she want to?

She had an overwhelming urge to march across the room and declare that she was a grown woman and therefore not involved in whatever games the lot of them were playing. A sharp prick snapped her attention back to her own table. Her sister had pinched her.

"Ow! Why'd you do that?" she asked, rubbing the spot on her forearm.

"Didn't you hear me say we don't have much time? And rather than snap to, you get this determined look on your face, and I know what that means."

"You do, huh?" Something about this entire day was bringing Riley right back to the days when they shared a room. She half expected her sister to throw out a "because Mom says" for good measure.

"That look means you are thinking of taking matters into your own hands. And I am here to tell you that will not work." Trish tapped her well-manicured fingers on the table. Riley pondered, as she often did when it came to Trish and herself, how two people could have the same upbringing and turn out so completely different.

For all Riley's corporate smarts and business savvy, Trish had the practicality and people skills. And beauty. Tricia Livingston was a strikingly beautiful woman, and though she carried herself well, she never seemed all that aware of it.

"Ri, you were smart enough to call me, now be smart enough to listen to what I have to say." The stretched smile relaxing for the briefest of moments to a more natural state, her voice softening.

Riley was about to object; she could feel her stubborn streak forming the words in her mouth. But before she could tell her sister exactly where she could put her so-called smart advice, a nervous-looking boy with a constellation of acne appeared beside their table. He was holding a ridiculously large mug filled with something topped with foam and smelling of cinnamon.

"I took the liberty of making your favorite latte, Mrs. Livingston." He smiled sheepishly as he set it on the table, never once looking Trish in the eye.

"That is too kind of you, Robbie," Trish purred, sliding the mug closer to her. "I can't believe you remembered!"

It was the tone of her voice more than anything else that finally caused something in Riley to concede. It was the same as the collective sound of those at the PTA meeting, and of the numerous phone calls she had received since. It was a tone she herself did not possess, and one that her new lot in life was going to force her to learn.

Trish was right. It was all in the nick of time.

As the blushing barista took his leave from the table, she acknowledged as much to her sister.

"Fine. You are right. I need you." She tilted her head to the side. "I have no idea how to deal with the pack of them."

"By the time we're through, you won't need to deal with them, sweetie. They'll be dealing with you."

"Don't think for a minute that what I am about to say means that I doubt you, but that would take a minor miracle."

Trish reached into the enormous brown satchel she had carried in and pulled out an overstuffed file. She laid it on the table and slid it toward Riley.

The sight of anything that looked remotely business-like—though the file folder was bright pink and covered in bright green paisley—piqued Riley's interest immediately. That there was something concrete in the folder sent a rush of joy through her. How in the world she thought the contents of a file could solve any of her problems left Riley more than a little perplexed. She furrowed her brow and flipped the folder so that the papers inside were facing her, and she began to read.

Hubbard School's Fourth Annual Fundraising Gala and Auction read the page on top, followed by a bullet-point list that Riley skimmed, still unsure how this was going to help her.

"Tricia, it's so good to see you! It has been ages." Cupcake had appeared beside their table with Screamer in tow.

"Boy, we sure do miss you." A nervous giggle escaped from Screamer's perfectly glossed pout of a mouth. She tried quickly to draw it back in but it caught in her throat. The result was an odd gagging sound that reminded Riley of the puppy accidentally inhaling bark from the twig he was gnawing on the night before.

This was definitely a lesson better observed than explained. Trish wrapped her hands around her mug, but she didn't smile. Riley leaned back, enjoying for a second the reversal of fortune the two women were experiencing.

"Thanks so much, Amy. My schedule seems to have gotten away from me, and I haven't had a minute to return any of your calls." Riley tried to keep her amusement from showing as Trish's nonchalant attitude toward her registered on Screamer's face.

"I've heard you are quite busy on the charity circuit nowadays," Cupcake added too brightly, dissolving into nervous giggles.

"We are just so hoping that we can pick your brain about the gala," Screamer chimed in.

Trish nodded. "Have you girls met my sister?" Ignoring Screamer's comment, Trish turned and smiled warmly in Riley's direction.

Riley perked up and attempted to fashion the smile she had seen on her sister's face when she arrived. Beside the table, the two women fell silent.

"I don't believe we've been formally introduced, no." Screamer replied, swallowing hard on what must have been a tiny little bit of her own pride.

Riley could barely contain her glee. "Riley Andrews." She extended her hand, and Cupcake took it, meekly, and shook it with all the vigor of a wet noodle.

Riley detested a wimpy handshake, but it didn't actually surprise her that Cupcake had one.

"Andrea Wexler," Cupcake said, her voice filled with what Riley now knew was "the tone."

"Amy Pixler." Screamer reached her hand across the table, but unlike her companion she made no attempt at nicety, apparently still holding a grudge over Riley's faux pas in the car line.

Riley shook her hand, being sure to give a grip so firm that Amy winced a bit. She turned to her sister. "I actually encountered Amy in the car line yesterday. I was a bit confused about the procedures."

Trish smiled that sweet, knowing smile.

"And did you do your PTA best to help my sister?" she queried, but then continued before Amy could answer. "I am just sure you did."

The statement hung in the air, awkwardly for Amy and Andrea, triumphantly for Riley and Trish. It was as sweet as the cinnamon latte that Trish brought to her mouth as they waited to see where the conversation would go next.

"So, about the gala," Amy sputtered, breaking the silence.

"Yes, we want to be sure to continue the tradition of your success," Andrea chimed in, a too-bright smile on her glossed lips.

"Well now, I don't think we will have to worry about that one bit, ladies." Trish waved a dismissive hand in the air as she concluded the conversation with a perfect tone, a perfect smile, and a perfect tilt of her head toward Riley, who sat stunned as the value of the file folder in front of her suddenly became all too clear. She flipped it closed and laid her hand on top of it, feeling as smug as she had ever been in her life.

She had what they wanted: Trish's master plan for a successful PTA gala. It was brilliant, and so, Riley realized for the first time in a long time, was her sister.

Chapter Seven

Sitting on her back porch, watching Ralph run around alternately chewing on twigs and peeing on trees, Riley felt an enormous sense of satisfaction. Not only did she give notice to the pack of PTA hyenas of her pedigree, but she actually had a plan to deal with them, on their own turf. If there was one thing Riley knew she could do, it was execute a plan.

The only thing horning in on her feeling of absolute joy was the phone call she needed to make to set the plan in motion. She looked down at the piece of paper in her hand. A warm flutter wafted through her stomach, replaced immediately by a quick stab of anxiety. No matter how pragmatic a matter it was, it was impossible for her to look at Sam's phone number without getting that one-two punch of emotions.

She needed a co-chair; Sam was the obvious choice. And it wasn't that she was nervous in the least about asking him. Pulling together a team of organized, effective people was one of the things she was known for in the advertising world. It was the way he had made her feel in their two brief encounters.

Her reaction to him was at odds with her current "hate all men" stance.

Riley was well aware that she hadn't actually had the opportunity to deal with her feelings about Daniel's leaving her. She was focused on Noah and their new life, and had not given herself time to mourn the life she'd lost. It was much easier to hate all men than to address how inadequate the whole thing made her feel.

But Sam had stirred exactly what she had banished. Something about him made her want to trust him. The soft crinkles around his eyes, the way he looked at Max, and the softness in his voice when he spoke of his son. There was an intense attraction to the man that Riley could not pretend didn't exist.

Squashing those thoughts, she focused on reality. It didn't matter what feelings he drummed up in her; he was a married man, and thus all of it was irrelevant. From a business perspective, she needed a co-chair, and he would be good at it. End of story.

She grabbed the phone that sat beside her and dialed his number, pleased that she was able to think logically. Making this phone call without a second thought was something she would have done in her old life, and that was something.

"Sam Aldin." His voice had a more professional tone about it too. Riley found this somehow reassuring.

"Sam, it's Riley Andrews," she replied, mirroring his confident, polished greeting.

"Riley, how are you?" The professional tone seemed to shift, and in its place came the familiarity they had established that day in the park.

The flutter in Riley's stomach was so evident she was sure the sound of a thousand wings could be heard through the tiny cell phone she pressed to her ear.

Focus on that band of gold.

"Good. Great, actually," she stammered, and then she squeezed her eyes shut to regain her focus. Irritation coursed through her veins. This was a professional call, and these wild emotions were getting the best of her. She cleared her throat.

"Listen, I'm calling because I have a plan and I'm hoping to include you."

There, that was more like it.

On the other end, Sam chuckled. Not exactly the kind of reaction she normally got when she was setting up a business proposal. But then again, no matter how she reasoned, nothing about this was normal from Riley's perspective, so she couldn't actually blame him. The last plan they'd executed together involved a plate of cookies and a quick escape from a room full of perfectly coiffed women.

"Does it involve staging a coup and overthrowing the reigning hierarchy of the Hubbard School PTA?"

"Not the entire hierarchy," she mused, relaxing into the conversation.

"Just parts of it, then?" He laughed.

"It's more about setting a new tone than about over-throwing them, I'd say."

"Well, Riley, I am intrigued, but I need to wrap some things up around here before Max gets home from school."

Riley checked her own watch, having a brief panic attack that she had somehow lost track of time, and poor Noah was sitting outside the school waiting for her to pick him up.

Two thirty. She had plenty of time.

God only knew what they did to the people who forgot their own children. Probably some sort of special detention where you're forced to write *I will never leave the house without showering* a thousand times.

"Okay. Well, do you want to give me a call back later this afternoon?"

"This afternoon is actually pretty tight. How about we do this face-to-face tomorrow, say lunch at Charlie's around twelve thirty?"

"Sure, that would be great," Riley heard herself say, followed by "I'll see you then." And while she was sure he had said something by way of good-bye, she couldn't remember actually hearing it.

She flipped her phone closed and tried to put what had just happened into a context that would quell the butterflies once and for all.

In order to find her way in the PTA, she was going to take over her sister's brainchild of a fundraiser. And with her sister backing her, there was no way any of those women would dare stop her from doing it. She needed a co-chair, because the amount of work was enormous, and Sam was the perfect, not to mention *only,* person in the PTA who she could work with, or rather who would work with her.

If all of this fell into place as she needed it to, there would be plenty of meetings, *professional* meetings that would include lunches, maybe even dinners. In the course of their working together, she would eventually meet his wife, and that would put an end to all this ridiculousness.

In fact, she was half-tempted to call him back and tell him to bring his wife to lunch to expedite the process. But that seemed a bit like overstepping her bounds.

The truth was, he was a nice guy who had shown her some kindness when she was completely overwhelmed. Any dime-store psychologist would say that she was merely enamored with him because of it.

She stood, feeling satisfied with her evaluation of the situation, and whistled for Ralph. Once this gala planning got rolling and she felt more in control, the whole thing would dissolve and someday she, Sam, and his wife would have a good laugh over it.

The puppy appeared from behind the garage, holding something in his mouth, and Riley clapped her hands for him to drop it. Ralph stopped dead in his tracks, and to her horror Riley could now see that what he held was not a stick or an old toy of Noah's, but some sort of small rodent. Normally, she was not girly about such things. She was, after all, substantially bigger than whatever Ralph was holding. But the mass of light gray fur protruding from the mouth of her new puppy gave Riley the creeps.

"Drop, it Ralph!" she commanded, but the puppy merely wagged his tail and continued toward her. It was obvious from the way the thing was moving that whatever it was, it was still alive, and headed right for her open back door.

"Ralph, no!"

But the dog would not be deterred, and before she knew it, he was up the porch steps and she had no choice but to grab his collar and try to keep him from getting inside. The sudden stop in his momentum caused Ralph to drop the thing; it hit the hard wood of the porch and began flailing around and emitting the most horrific noise Riley had ever heard. It righted itself and waved its odd front paws in a swimming motion.

The animal was a baby mole. Blind as it was, it would never make its way off her back porch. To make matters worse, Ralph was straining at his collar, trying desperately to get another crack at the thing.

Struggling, she managed to drag the yelping puppy into the house. Next, she grabbed for the broom, ready to sweep the thing back into the grass and be done with the whole mess. But then she paused and thought about how much damage that one blind little rodent could do to her lawn. Not sure what to do next, she grabbed a bucket from the pantry and ran back outside only to discover that the creature had managed to roll off the porch and was frantically digging a hole in her yard.

Armed only with the bucket, she scooped at it. The lip of the bucket brushed the grass, and she felt a bump that made her think she had captured the thing. But she didn't anticipate the forward motion of the bucket, and instead of capturing the mole, she instead sent it flying through the air, across the fence and into the backyard of her neighbor, an angry old woman named Mrs. Schultz who regularly berated Riley for leaving her garbage cans on the curb after collection day.

Riley waited, praying the old woman was nowhere near her yard or a window when the poor hapless mole came flying through the air. But after a few seconds, with no obvious reaction, she breathed a sigh of relief.

Problem solved, mole removed.

As ridiculous as the whole scene was, she had solved a domestic problem on her own, and it was very satisfying.

The alert on her BlackBerry sounded, and checking her watch she saw that it was time to pick up Noah. Maybe she could manage this whole domestic thing after all. Feeling quite pleased with herself, she climbed into her car and backed down the driveway.

The song on the radio was upbeat, she knew the words, and as she drove the short distance to the school, she opened the sunroof and sang along, feeling a lightness she hadn't felt in weeks. She would conquer the PTA, master this domesticity, maybe even befriend Sam's wife. They must have a lot in common if he was the main PTA parent, Riley reasoned. She hadn't thought of that while she was mooning over the poor woman's husband.

As if on cue, the phone beside her rang, and she smiled to see Sam's number on the display.

"Are you in the car line?" she asked, pulling her own car into the pick-up line in front of the school.

"Just pulled out," he said, then added, "so don't run anyone down, because you don't have any backup."

Riley laughed, a real laugh, not the nervous giggle she had been prone to only an hour earlier, when they had last spoken.

"Listen, I can't do lunch tomorrow after all."

"Oh, that's too bad. I was actually looking forward to it." Her eyes stayed locked on the car in front of her, watching for taillights as her foot hovered over her own brake pedal.

"How about you and Noah come over to our house for dinner instead?"

"That would be wonderful!" she exclaimed, her car inching closer to the front, her mind focused on braking at the right moment.

"Great. I'll e-mail you the address. How about around six so the boys can eat at a regular time?"

"Perfect. See you then."

Her car pulled even with the front entrance of the

school, and she pressed down on the brakes and searched the crowd for the familiar face of her son.

It was perfect. She would meet Mrs. Aldin and put an end to her emotional nonsense, and they would all hatch their plan to bring sanity back to the Hubbard PTA. Things were getting on track, just as she knew they would. All it took was a little planning, and reason.

Noah bounded out of the crowd of kids. In a jumble of backpack, lunch bag, and eight-year-old enthusiasm, he piled into the backseat, already telling her about his day before he even buckled his seat belt. Riley was filled with an overwhelming sense of contentment.

Chapter Eight

Why are they coming to dinner?" Max asked as he clumsily carried a stack of dishes to the table. The rattle and clatter as he set them down caused Sam to look up from chopping vegetables at the counter. The furrow in his son's brow as he placed his small hands on top of the stack to steady them tugged at the edges of Sam's heart.

"Mrs. Andrews and I are in the PTA together. And she and Noah are coming to dinner because I thought it would be nice for us to start making some friends here in town."

It was a logical enough reason to have invited them to dinner, and it was true, in part. The decision to extend the invitation had taken Sam a bit by surprise even as he'd been extending it. His growing fascination with Riley Andrews both intrigued and alarmed him. Having them over for dinner and establishing more of a friendship, he hoped, would help him get a better grip on the effect Riley had on him.

64

"I like Noah," Max announced as he made his way around the table, arranging the dishes and silverware. "Do you think they'll bring Ralph?"

"I'm guessing they won't, but maybe we can arrange to meet up with them in the park again sometime." Sam went back to methodically chopping the vegetables for the pasta he was making for dinner.

Cooking was something he and Maggie had enjoyed doing together almost from the moment they met. She had cooked for him on their first date, and he had returned the favor on their second. While other couples did their courting in the nice restaurants and trendy sushi joints in the city, they had settled into a slightly competitive cooking contest that became the foundation of their relationship.

When they got married and then Max came along, they vowed that he would not be a kid who ate only chicken nuggets and hot dogs. As a result, he had a taste for things like Chilean sea bass and rosemary potatoes. Tonight, however, Sam was playing it safe with a pasta primavera and garlic bread, figuring at the very least Noah would eat the noodles and bread if he found the vegetables offensive.

He was toying with yet another reason he had invited Riley to dinner—telling her about Maggie. Eventually the story of his late wife would get out. Somehow, having Riley know before anyone else made sense to Sam, as if he were testing the waters with someone he thought would be sincerely sympathetic to his loss. He also preferred she find out from him and not someone who would treat the news as a bit of gossip.

Telling her seemed like a good thing to do, but once the story was out, there was no getting it back. There was something about the look on Riley's face that first day that made him believe she would understand, and true sincerity was something he rarely saw.

"He's at my recess too."

"Hmm?" Sam was lost in his own thoughts and thus gave Max the response that caused him the most fatherly guilt—the verbal cue that he wasn't truly listening to what his son was saying.

"Yeah. We play on the monkey bars. He doesn't like kickball, either." Max crossed the kitchen and tugged on his dad's sleeve, a clear indicator that he knew Sam wasn't really listening.

Sam sighed, put down the small paring knife he was holding, and turned so his son knew he had his full attention.

"Sounds like you two have a lot in common," he said, running his hand over his son's blond head.

A serious look came across the boy's face, the same one that had haunted them both during the months that Maggie was sick and the time right after. It cut Sam to the quick, and he knelt in front of his son.

"What is it, buddy?"

Max looked down at his fingers and picked at a hangnail.

"It's just," he stammered, then raised his eyes to meet

the intent look from his father. "I like that the kids at school don't know about Mom. No one is sad when they look at me. They just want to be my friend, like Noah. I don't want people to know yet." Tears pooled in his hazel eyes, his mother's eyes.

Sam pulled his son into his arms, the weight of him throwing off his balance, and they fell awkwardly onto the kitchen floor.

"I know what you mean," he said, his mind floating back to just moments earlier when he had been toying with the idea of telling Riley.

"Do you feel bad too?" It was a most innocent question, and Max had pulled away so that he could look at Sam.

"Bad?"

"About not wanting to tell people about Mom? Like I don't want to remember her or something." His voice was tinged with the tears that now tumbled down his cheeks.

Sam felt another piece of his heart break, as it always did when he saw Max in tears.

"Max, all your mom ever wanted was for you to be the happiest boy you could be. And if that means keeping her death to ourselves, it's not forgetting her. It's doing what she would have wanted."

Relief flooded the boy's face and almost seemed to overflow into Sam as he felt his own sorrow wash away in the gleam in his son's eye.

"Promise?"

"Promise," Sam said, pulling Max tight, happy to have the answer the boy was looking for, knowing that wouldn't always be the case.

The doorbell rang, breaking the moment and thrusting them back into the duties at hand.

Max jumped up and raced for the door. Sam stood, wiped his hands on the dish towel he'd slung over his shoulder, glad for the moment they had shared. As much as he wanted to tell Riley about his late wife, he knew he couldn't. As it had so many times in the last year, Max's happiness meant more to Sam than anything else.

He followed his son down the narrow hall to the front door, which Max had already opened.

"Come on in," his son practically squealed. Sam felt a rush of assurance that this dinner was the right thing to have done, regardless of how intrigued he was by Riley, or his sudden decision not to tell her about Maggie.

"Yes, come on in," he echoed, reaching around Max to open the screen door. Noah rushed passed him, and the boys raced off in the direction of Max's room. Sam and Riley, alone in the foyer, smiled broadly at their sons' enthusiasm.

"It's a shame those two are so shy around each other," Sam quipped, closing the door behind Riley as she stepped inside.

"Isn't it?" The smile remained on Riley's face and Sam noted a twinkle in her eye that hadn't been there the last few times they'd seen each other. It suited her, though he found her usual look of annoyed bewilderment equally attractive.

"I brought ice cream," she said holding up a brown paper bag. "I wanted to bring something, and I knew you and Noah liked it, but I wasn't sure about your wife, so I hope it's all right."

"My wife?" he repeated, the promise to Max still ringing in his ears. But the uncertainty of what to say about his wife's whereabouts caused him to pause. Sam was not a dishonest person.

"Yes, your wife," Riley looked past him toward the kitchen. "I can't wait to meet her. Based on your PTA participation, I think she and I will have a lot in common." A sheepish smile crossed her face, and Sam understood immediately.

Riley thought Maggie was a career woman and that was why he was so active in Max's school. The story was already formulated in her mind. All he had to do was agree with it. That didn't technically qualify as lying, he reasoned to himself. It was for Max, after all.

"Actually, she isn't going to be able to join us tonight," he said lightly, reaching for the bag Riley held in her hand, and indicating she should follow him toward the kitchen.

"Oh, that's too bad," Riley said, her voice ringing true to her disappointment. "Hung up at work?"

"Something like that," Sam replied, his guilt over misleading her churning in his head. He opened the freezer and stuck the bag inside. Then, in an attempt to keep busy while the half-truths hung in the air, he opened the fridge and pulled out a bottle of wine.

"Drink?" he asked, holding it up so she could see it, and with her nod, he turned and bent to open the cool green bottle.

"Next time, I guess," she said, and he could hear from behind that she had taken over setting the table where Max had left off.

If only, he thought. A crushing sense of loss flooded him, and he put his hands on the countertop to steady himself.

"Sam, is something wrong?" Riley asked, her voice filled with the sincere concern that he had expected to hear when he told her about Maggie. Until that very moment, he hadn't realized how much he had wanted to hear it in Riley's voice. For the first time since Maggie's death, he had wanted some heartfelt kindness from a woman.

Suddenly, he was very glad he had promised Max he wouldn't tell. Something about Riley Andrews had awakened a part of him that he thought had died with his wife. And that reality was as overwhelming as the tears that had fallen from the eyes of his son.

Chapter Nine

Okay, so sit in the third row. Not the first; that's where the kiss-ups sit, and not in the back, because that's where the warm bodies congregate." Trish's voice buzzed in Riley's ear. She was on her way to the granddaddy of all PTA meetings, committee sign-ups. And despite being well armed, she was still a bit apprehensive.

The entire thing was beginning to feel more like junior high kids storming the cool table than caring, involved parents working toward a good school for their children. She had expressed as much to Trish at the start of their phone call and had been told in no uncertain terms that it was *exactly* like junior high, though the stakes were much higher.

Riley wanted more than anything not to have to do as she was told, but she wanted to be there for Noah, and this was apparently how it was done. As ridiculous as it was.

"Warm bodies. Do I even want to know?" she asked her sister.

71

"The women who sit in the back sign up for nothing, end up doing all the work, and get no credit for any of it."

At least that made sense. It was the same in the advertising world: if you wanted to get anywhere, people had to know your name and the quality of work you could deliver. Riley lived for the moments when the life she was living now was even slightly similar to her work experience.

Those moments were fleeting. She was doing her best to run things the way she had at the office, but the two didn't always mesh. Who knew one little red sock in hot water would turn an entire load of white towels pink? Some days, it felt like there were just too many things she needed to learn.

"That's the first thing you've said that makes any sort of normal sense," Riley replied quickly. "I'm pulling into the school now, so wrap it up."

Trish sighed heavily, and Riley pulled the phone away from the annoying static on her end of the call.

"Fine. When you get there, sit in the third row, but when they start sending the clipboards around for sign-up, the gala will be last, and then you stand up, announce your intention to chair the committee, and put your hand out for the sheet."

"And if Cupcake and Screamer won't hand it over?"

"Oh, they'll hand it over. The pecking order of that group of hens is very clear, and they won't cross me. And by me, I mean you, of course."

"Of course," Riley repeated absently, feeling the exact same way she had felt on her first day of work.

"So, take no prisoners, and call me when it's over!"

"Believe me, you'll be the first person on my list. Thanks! Bye!" Riley snapped her phone closed.

She glanced around the parking lot, full of SUVs and minivans, the PTA moms streaming into the school like ants when you pour water on their hill. She dreaded it. Dreaded going into a meeting of know-it-alls when she knew nothing. Even with her plan in motion, even with Sam on her side, even with Trish pulling the strings with her giant secret file of galas past, she dreaded it.

But it didn't matter, because she had to go. Failure was not an option in any aspect of her life, loser husband aside, of course.

Suddenly, Riley was very aware that she was just sitting in her car staring out the window at the other moms, and how that might look to all of them. She picked up the file on the passenger seat and thumbed through it, using the first rule of business—even if you aren't sure exactly what is going on, pretend that you are.

When a reasonable amount of time had passed, she snapped the file closed and was surprised to see two moms waving at her through her windshield. Perfect smiles plastered on their faces, they greeted her with the enthusiasm of a homecoming queen leading a parade. Surely they mistook her for someone else, and she almost pointed to herself and mouthed "me?" but then thought better of it and waved back.

Their smiles widened, and they literally skipped off toward the front of the school, leaving Riley to wonder what bizarro world she had entered. Climbing out of her car, she didn't have to wonder long.

"It's so good to see you this morning, Riley!" The enthusiastic voice made her turn swiftly, feeling like the new convict in the prison yard who had to watch for the shank. She was barely surprised to be face-to-face with Cupcake.

"Good to see you too, Cup . . . er . . . Andrea, isn't it?" She plastered what she thought was a perfect PTA smile on her face to cover the obvious faux pas of forgetting the woman's name, and started walking toward the entrance.

The woman fell in step with her, keeping up the brisk pace set by Riley's determination and long stride.

"Yes, it is Andrea!" she exclaimed, so thrilled Riley remembered her name that the pitch of her voice vibrated Riley's eardrums.

"So, you want to sit together?"

"Um, well," Riley stammered, trying to remember exactly where she was supposed to sit and why. They rounded the corner, and, mercifully, she was saved from answering the question by Sam, who was sitting on the bench by the front door waiting for her.

"I would love to, but I need to speak with Sam real quick," she said, tilting her head, as Trish had taught her to do when she was dismissing someone. "You go on in, and I'll be right behind you."

"Super!"

"So," Riley said, turning her attention to Sam, swallowing hard, "you ready for this?"

"It's committee sign-ups. Super!" He waved his hands in the air to feign mock excitement.

Riley rolled her eyes. "I would agree with you, but apparently there's a whole thing about where we need to sit, and how the clipboards are passed, and when we need to stand up . . ."

His smile broadened as she spoke, and Riley tried hard to equate the uptick in her pulse to nerves over the coup they were staging.

"Just follow my lead. I don't have time to explain it all," she said as confidently as she could, and she pulled hard on the door that would take them into the school and the meeting.

They entered the crowded cafeteria, the site of her last fateful PTA meeting, but this time it was quite a different scene. The roar of the crowd seemed to heighten as they entered. Instead of the furrowed brows and scowls that greeted her the last time, there were broad smiles and wide-eyed staring.

"Good morning, Riley!" exclaimed a tubby little woman she recognized from the coffeehouse.

"Good morning," Riley replied, her voice a mixture of utter confusion and forced confidence.

"I'm sure glad to see you this morning," came another, this one accompanied by a pat on her arm.

Sam leaned forward and whispered in her ear, his

warm breath tickling her already heightened senses. "Did someone spike the coffee? And if so, where do I get some?"

Riley smiled and tipped her head back, almost leaning on his shoulder to reply. "Nope. It would seem that the word is out about my family PTA connections." She smiled at the gaggle of women sitting tall in the front row who waved in unison.

"Who knew the Hubbard School PTA was so much like the Mafia?" Sam chortled and Riley caught her own laughter before it escaped. Of all the ridiculous things she had heard in the past few weeks, that was actually the most accurate.

"Ladies, if you could all find a seat." A loud, clear voice above the din instructed them, and a hush fell over the room as the women scurried to do as they were told.

"And gentleman, of course."

At the mention of the man in their midst, the room filled with as much twitter as a group of thirteen-year-olds.

Riley was more than slightly embarrassed for them, though her insides seemed to twitter every time she and Sam were in close proximity.

But this was not the time to think about that; she had to focus. She strode toward the third row of chairs, but before she could reach her destination, a woman stepped in front of her. Suddenly, Riley found herself nose to nose with the PTA president, Stephanie Ann Growsler.

Of course she had two first names; what self-respecting PTA president didn't?

Their eyes met, and the woman's gaze was steely. She nodded slightly. It was clear to Riley that Stephanie Ann saw her as a threat. This was an attempt at intimidation. But it wouldn't work.

A power struggle was another thing Riley's corporate life had prepared her for, along with how to win one.

Game on.

"Good morning," she said, her voice clear and without waver. Then she stepped around the woman and walked with confidence to the third row, where she took her seat. Sam followed suit.

He leaned in to whisper to her, and his warm breath on her ear sent shivers up the back of her neck. The whispering had to stop; it was muddling her thoughts.

"Rowr!"

She shot him a look and he chuckled silently.

"I'm just saying I see a cat fight in the making," he whispered again.

Riley turned to face him, irritation mixed with the rush of heat from his warm breath on her ear.

"Why is it that men always equate strong women challenging one another with a cat fight?" she snapped, irritated with both the sexist remark and herself for letting a married man stir these sorts of feelings in her.

Sam scrunched his face into a look of mock confusion and shrugged his shoulders as a sly smile spread across his face. He was opening his mouth to say something, but before the words could form there was a loud clap, and they turned to see that the meeting was being called to order.

As Stephanie Ann spoke, Riley's mind raced, trying to get back to the fierce professional place she had been before Sam distracted her with his warm, sweet-smelling breath and sparkling blue eyes. It was supposed to be about finding her place, claiming her territory. Instead, as much as she hated to admit it, not only was the PTA being run like a junior high clique, but her feelings for Sam were growing. It was a situation as impossible as a band nerd falling for the star football player.

He's married. He's married.

She repeated that over and over to herself as Stephanie Ann droned on. Riley wasn't listening. She had to start focusing on the task at hand. Her heart beat faster and faster, drowning out all outside words. She needed to get out of that room, away from Sam. She needed to get a grip, but she could do none of those things until she'd signed up to chair the God-forsaken gala.

At last, the clipboards appeared. And though she had no idea what the president was saying about them the memory of what Trish had instructed her to do allowed Riley to leap to her feet and declare, "I would like to chair the gala, and Sam has agreed to be my co-chair."

A still silence fell over the room, and the steely glare from the president was far more Cold War than cat fight. Nevertheless, Riley held her ground, her hand extended for the clipboard.

From where she stood, it didn't seem as though Stephanie Ann was going to give it up. But Riley held her position.

"We've never had a first-year PTA member with no experience plan our biggest event," Stephanie Ann said icily.

"Oh, I have experience, just not in this venue," Riley replied.

"That is what worries me," Stephanie Ann shot back. "You aren't familiar with the way we do things here in the Hubbard School PTA."

And though she could think of a million replies, none of which were the least bit productive or appropriate, Riley was saved from answering by the entrance of the one person no one in the PTA wanted to look bad in front of: Principal Jones.

"Good morning, PTA!" he chirped.

"Good morning."

The reply was less than enthusiastic. Riley sensed that the crowd was annoyed with the interruption, waiting to see what might happen next. It dawned on Riley, as she stood there and surveyed the room, how stacked the deck was against the working parent. The Hubbard School PTA held their business meetings during the day, and no working parent could possibly attend all of them. She glanced at Sam, who she knew was able to set his own hours, but he was the exception rather than the rule. The unfairness fueled her desire to run the gala even more and prove her worth, the worth of the career woman.

"What are we discussing this morning?" he asked, placing his hands on his hips and surveying the scene.

Riley knew this was probably her best shot at getting what she wanted.

"Sam and I have just volunteered to co-chair the Winter Gala," she announced, smiling broadly at the principal before turning her gaze to Stephanie Ann.

Her adversary's eyes flared in anger, but Stephanie Ann said nothing. To turn down a volunteer in front of the principal, with no reason other than the pecking order of the PTA, would not look good.

And looking bad was a cardinal sin in the PTA.

Her shoulders drooped a bit, and she crossed the room to hand the sign-up sheet to Riley.

"That is tremendous news!" Principal Jones clapped his hands. "A school is only as strong as its parent volunteers!" he continued, clapping, and the others in the room joined in, sparsely at first, but then with thundering noise.

Amid the raucous noise of the group, Stephanie Ann took the opportunity to make her true feelings known.

"This isn't over," she said tightly, shoving the clipboard at Riley.

And as she took it, Riley knew that to be true. But she also knew she had won round one.

Chapter Ten

Are you kidding me? Principal Jones himself backed you to head up the Winter Gala? That's unheard of!" Trish's voice held a hint of actual envy, and Riley was tempted to bask in it a bit, if it wasn't such a ridiculous thing to envy.

Though besting her perfect sister at anything, at this point in Riley's life, did hold a small amount of satisfaction.

"I don't know if he actually knew he was weighing in on something controversial," Riley countered, sliding her coat off as she juggled the phone on her shoulder. She was starving, having skipped breakfast in order to be on time for the meeting. She had a sneaking suspicion there wasn't much to be found in her refrigerator.

Well, more than a suspicion—it was a concrete fact. Ever since the grocery shopping became part of her job description, she and Noah, on more than one occasion, had had to run out at the last minute for ingredients.

"It seemed to me he was just trying to get some face

time with the PTA and then get the heck out of there. He's a professional, after all. I would think he would have much more important things to do than involve himself with the politics of these women," she said, seizing the last bruised apple in the fruit bowl and taking a bite.

The silence from the other end of the phone was deafening. Riley let it be for a moment or two, chewing her apple, before she started to wonder what had caused it.

"Trish? You still there? Did I lose you?"

"Riley, I know you can't help who you are, but you did ask for my help, so I have to tell you. The condescending way you throw that word around isn't going to get you anywhere."

"What word?" Riley could feel her eyes rolling, but did her best to stop them. Even though they were on the phone and Trish couldn't possibly know she was getting the roll, it was still good practice for when they were face to face.

"Professional."

Riley bit the inside of her cheek and pressed her eyes closed tight. This was familiar ground between them. A discussion they had had many, many times.

"I didn't mean anything by it. The man is an education professional. He has a degree, probably an advanced one, in something he is paid to do," she said, hoping that the lame explanation would do the trick and they could move on without the usual lengthy discussion and disagreement.

"I'm not an idiot, Riley! I do know what the word means!" Trish exhaled loudly, as though she was trying to regain her famed composure. "It's the *way* you say it. It's so patronizing. You just might want to think about that."

Riley's ears grew hot, and not just the one pressed to her phone. She tried to reason through her next comment. There was a great deal she had to say on the subject, but she feared that doing so would alienate her sister to the point of not helping her, and she needed the help, desperately.

Time and place, time and place.

It was something she often chanted in her head when she was trying to keep from shooting herself in the foot. It was her mantra of meditation. That, combined with some deep breaths and a rant or two to a sympathetic ear at a later date.

"I will think about it," Riley said in a voice she hoped held no trace of her irritation.

"Okay, then." Trish's surprise at her easy victory was evident.

"Okay, then," Riley repeated, making her way to the pantry and looking for anything that would satisfy her hunger. Finding nothing, she took another bite of the apple, trying to ignore its mealy texture.

"So, when are you and your co-chair available to meet with me?"

"I'll check with Sam, but for now, why don't you plan on dinner tonight?"

"I don't think a restaurant is a great idea at this point. We need to try and keep my involvement under wraps for the moment, or all the credit will just go to me."

"I agree. Why don't we do it here? Then we can spread everything out on the dining room table and make a sort of war room."

Already she had visions of transforming the seldom-used dining space into a corporate-style conference room, with flip charts taped to the walls and files and notebooks littering the table. The parallel made her tingle a bit.

"Dinner, at your house?"

Riley's grasp on her half-eaten apple tightened. Trish was certainly exercising her high-maintenance qualities today. And while Riley was the first to admit cooking anything was not her strong suit, she had had all she could take of Saint Trish of the gilded homemakers society for the moment.

"Chinese take-out, if that's okay with you."

"Not my favorite, but it's better than rolling the dice with your cooking. See you about seven!"

And she was gone, leaving Riley, who had begun the call elated, seething on the now-dead phone she still held to her ear.

"Time and place," she said aloud to her empty house. The puppy asleep in the corner raised his head at the sound of her voice but then lowered it sleepily back to his pillow.

"Time and place!" she said even louder, feeling no better for it.

Pacing the floor of the kitchen, she bit savagely into the apple, until nothing was left but the core and her irritation. If only Trish could be slightly less condescending, it would help.

Wasn't it enough that she got to tell Riley exactly what to do and Riley was actually doing it? Did she have to present their every conversation as though she was the sensei and Riley was the Karate Kid?

And if this was the way the whole thing was going to proceed, how in the world was she going to get through it without creating a greater rift between her and Trish? Was the prize really worth the psychological pain and suffering she was about to endure?

She needed part two of her meditation—the rant portion.

Flipping her phone open, she punched the numbers with fervor, not hesitating in the least.

"Hello?"

"Sam, it's Riley."

"I assumed I'd be getting a call, after your showdown this morning."

"This is more about my sister than the meeting. I invited her over for dinner tonight, to go over things for this gala. I'm hoping that not only will you be able to come and buffer, but maybe you can come a wee bit earlier so that I can vent a bit before she gets here?"

"That's quite an invitation—one of the more original I've ever received. And one I can't possibly resist. What time?"

"Let's say six." Riley felt her anger subsiding and her appreciation for her new friend growing.

"See you then!" he said cheerfully as he hung up.

Riley did the same, and only then did she realize she hadn't invited his wife, hadn't even thought to ask about her. And while she could justify it by putting it all on the drama her sister had introduced into the situation, the truth was that, in the moment, she had completely forgotten he had a wife.

"And that," she said, bending over to rub the ears of the still sleeping puppy, "isn't good!"

Ralph sighed, and Riley, beleaguered by it all, could only think to do the same.

Chapter Eleven

When the doorbell rang, Riley made a mental note *not* to check her reflection in the hall mirror, as a woman might when she was opening the door for a man with whom she was having a date, even though she had spent the better part of her late afternoon primping as though that was exactly what she was doing that very evening.

But this was not a date; it was a business meeting.

She justified her primping by telling herself that she was merely taking care of some maintenance she had overlooked in the hectic pace of her new lifestyle. Kind of like how she overlooked the empty fridge and the piles of laundry—things she should really make a priority.

Eyebrow plucking, clarifying masque, deep hair conditioning, and even a quick run over her nails with a file had all fallen into this category. And though she knew her excuse was feeble, it had been a long time since she had paid any attention to even the basics of her appearance. She found she rather enjoyed taking care of herself again.

Noah entertained himself on the floor of her bedroom with a box of Legos, his constant chatter the background noise as she brushed her hair and ran a bit of blush over her cheekbones. The sounds of his happy play danced around the room and lifted her spirits to the extent that she was beginning to think she didn't even need to rant about Trish.

"Is Max coming over with his dad?" Noah asked, his small hands expertly attaching one small block to another.

"You know, buddy, I'm not really sure."

She had wondered herself, but then quickly conjured up a scenario in which Max was staying home with his mother and thus justifying her failure to invite the woman to dinner.

Cue the doorbell.

"I'll get it!" Noah yelled, scrambling up from the pile of blocks on the floor, the ones in his lap dropping like confetti as he raced out of the room.

"Early. Perfect," Riley said to herself, smiling in anticipation.

What happened next did little to calm the sudden burst of nerves the doorbell had ignited.

"Daddy!"

Daddy?

"Noah!" was the reply, and in an instant her soon-to-be ex had stepped inside what used to be his home and swept their son up in a bear hug. His face, staring directly at her over the top of the boy's head, was expressionless. There was not a trace of nerves or embarrassment, as though it was perfectly natural to show up unannounced to see the family he had so readily abandoned.

Riley could feel her nerves give way to something more like red-hot anger combined with what she was sure a mother bear must feel when her cub wanders into a campsite.

"Daniel, what an unexpected surprise," she said, making sure to keep her tone even as not to concern Noah.

"Yeah. I was in the neighborhood and had an idea that maybe I could take Noah out for some pizza!"

He held the boy back as he said it, and Riley took note of the broad smile that broke across her son's face.

She couldn't ignore it. Couldn't put her own feelings of anger and resentment, which bordered on hatred, ahead of the love her son felt for his father. Doing so would make her no better than the man.

"Does that sound good to you, Noah?" she asked, ignoring Daniel altogether.

"Only if it's Tower Pizza," he said, turning and posing his question to his father.

"Whatever you want, buddy. And of course you are more than welcome to join us, Riley," he said, setting Noah back on the ground.

The invitation was as unexpected as his arrival. As she fought back the urge to tell him exactly what he could do with it, she was saved by her adorable son.

"Oh, Mom can't come. She's having Sam over for dinner."

"Sam?" Daniel asked, and Riley was pleased to see a look of interest cross his expressionless face despite herself.

"Sam is a friend of mine from the PTA." Her answer was honest; her voice was even; her intention was to keep him guessing.

"I don't remember a Samantha from the PTA," Daniel pushed on, missing her obvious insinuation that whatever she might be doing was none of his business.

"Samantha is a girl's name," Noah said, giggling in a way that only an eight-year-old can at such a mix-up. "Sam is a boy."

Daniel stared at her, his eyes suddenly narrow and hard. "A boy, huh?"

"Okay, Noah, why don't you go grab your shoes and a jacket?"

"Right away!" he squealed, and he ran down the hall, leaving the two of them alone.

"So, try to have him back by eight so he can get to bed on time," Riley said, choosing to ignore the elephant in the room.

"Just so I'm clear about what is going on, you have a date tonight?" Daniel's tone was a cross between interrogation and disbelief. He was ignoring her attempt to smooth the whole thing over, and with that, the slight grasp she held on her irritation was broken.

"Just so *I'm* clear, I don't think it's any of your darn

business what's going on here if it doesn't have to do with Noah."

She stared into his eyes, knowing her face was flushed and her own eyes were flaring the full extent of her anger. Riley was a woman who seldom lost control. Perhaps that was the biggest source of frustration in her current situation—she had no control over any of it.

Moreover, the root of all her problems had showed up out of nowhere, as if he were father of the year, extending pizza invitations!

She expected his reaction to be one of anger, but instead he let out a knowing laugh.

"Being a PTA dad is like being a rooster in a henhouse. All the ladies clamor for your attention. Pouring their hearts out about how they wish their husbands were as involved as you. Yes, being the only man in the PTA had its benefits, that's for sure."

He lifted his chin ever so slightly, and though she knew he was just hitting back at her, the insinuation that he had been a shoulder for any of those women while she was off at work, believing in him and their marriage, made her blood boil.

"I just never thought you'd be the kind of woman who would fall prey to that sort of thing."

She knew him well enough to know that he was saying these things out of his own hurt feelings, but it still sent her spinning.

And she was tired of spinning.

"Just try to have Noah home by eight so that he can

get to bed on time, please," she repeated. Then, without waiting for his response, she turned to help Noah with his shoes and coat.

She found him sitting on the floor in the mudroom struggling to tie his sneakers, the smile still there, the knots in his laces the direct result of his excitement about seeing his dad. Taking a deep breath to compose herself, she knelt down and began to untangle the mess.

"Are you sure you can't come? You love Pizza Tower, Mommy."

Looping the strings and pulling them tight, she looked up into her son's happy face and shook her head.

"Nope. This is your time with Daddy. Besides, Sam is coming over, and we have work to do for your school, remember?"

He nodded as he jumped to his feet, grabbed his hoodie off the peg above his head, and scampered down the hall.

"Ready!" he called, and Riley could hear his giggles as she followed him back to where she had left Daniel just moments earlier.

Those giggles, that smile—they were what she had to focus on now. Not how much comfort Daniel had given to the PTA moms or her humiliation at his leaving her. Not how much she wanted to make him think her dinner with Sam was more then just a meeting about a stupid fundraiser.

"You two have some fun boy time," she said with true sincerity and what she hoped was a bright smile.

"I'm glad Sam is coming over, so you don't have to be lonely without me, Mommy."

Noah smiled, and she bent down to hug him good-bye before shuffling them out her front door.

"Yes, you and Sam have a great night. We'll be back at eight," Daniel said over his shoulder as he followed Noah out the door.

And just like that, her attempt to take the high road was clouded over by the satisfaction she felt at Daniel's obvious jealousy. A little personal pleasure couldn't hurt as long as she kept it to herself, she reasoned as she watched them pull away from the curb in Daniel's new sports car.

As if it were scripted in a movie, their exit was followed by Sam's entrance as he pulled into her driveway.

It's like a carousel of characters—each one designed to elicit another emotion, Riley thought, as she held on to the porch railing to steady herself for what might come next.

Chapter Twelve

Your timing is impeccable!" Riley called as Sam climbed out of his car, shooting her a smile that warmed her from the inside.

He was dressed in jeans and a dark green hooded sweatshirt, but somehow he managed to avoid looking as though he was dressed as either a college kid or an old man.

"Were you going to start the ranting without me?" He crossed the yard, his eyes twinkling as he teased her lightly. "You know, there are experts who say ranting to oneself is the first sign of insanity."

In her old life, Riley had despised being teased. She found it irritating, and she firmly believed that teasing was just a way for people to express what they really thought of you. It seemed to her that if someone had something to say, they could just come right out and say it. But when Sam did it, it seemed like he was just trying to open her eyes to a different way of looking at something, and maybe get her to lighten up and laugh at herself a bit.

And though it was extremely hard for Riley to admit that her way was not the only way, it was more than obvious that she needed some perspective from someone other than Trish.

"I think you're fine as long as you know you're crazy. It's when you start claiming to be sane that you're in trouble."

He laughed, and for the first time that day, Riley did the same. All of it—the PTA meeting, her oversensitive sister, her reappearing husband—was insane. It was either laugh or cry, and seeing the delighted grin on Sam's face, Riley was confident that she had made the right choice.

She turned, opened the screen door, and led the way into the house, down the hall, and into the kitchen, where she plopped down in a chair.

"I thought better of bringing Max," Sam said as he sat down across from her at the table. "I assumed this was going to be a working dinner and might run past his bedtime. I hope Noah won't be too disappointed."

"Well, he would have been, but he just left. He went with his dad for pizza at the last minute." Riley kept her tone light, as though this was just as fine as could be. She glanced down at her hands as she spoke, however, finding she couldn't look him in the eye.

Rubbing her thumb over the top of her knuckles, she

pondered the moment of silence, and glanced up to find Sam staring intently at her.

There was a vulnerability in Riley that Sam had never seen before as she sat there fiddling with her fingers, not looking him in the eye. There was more to it than just pizza, but he wasn't one to force a confidence. Still, he found himself fighting the urge to slide his chair closer to hers and wrap his arms around her. He was well aware that his feelings for Riley were intense, and growing. And while it didn't cause him apprehension, he knew their situation was already complicated—her newly single status, their sons, the fact that she still thought he had a wife, and his promise to Max to keep it that way.

So, instead, he simply nodded his head and hoped the urge would pass and he could get the conversation back to a more neutral topic, like the PTA and this sister of hers.

"So, your sister? The PTA? Noah's dad? Where do you want to start?"

Just like that, the vulnerability vanished. When Riley looked up, her eyes blazed with the fiery attitude he had come to expect.

"A conversation spent on Noah's dad would be a waste of both of our time."

"How so?"

Riley's eyebrows raised ever so slightly, as though

she was purposely clearing her mind of whatever effect the man had on her.

"In a nutshell, and without boring you with the details of my failed marriage, he set the ground rules for our relationship, decided they didn't work for him, and then left. He was like a trifecta of the qualities I most despise in a person: controlling, unreliable, and dishonest." She gave a curt nod, clearly indicating it was all she was going to say on the subject. Sam swallowed, not having anything to respond with after such a succinct account of a complex situation.

"All right. So, how about your sister, then?" he stammered, hoping this was better subject matter.

"My sister! Yes, before she gets here, because Lord knows I can't pick a fight with her!"

"You, scared of picking a fight with someone, after your standoff with President Stephanie Ann this morning? I can't imagine you being intimidated."

Riley rolled her eyes. "Please, I am not intimidated by Trish! I am just very aware I need her help at this moment in my life. I would love more than anything to tell her just what she can do with that help, but I would essentially be hurting myself. And, as I already pointed out, I'm way too smart to do that."

"If you're so smart, what am I doing here?" Sam egged her on.

"You are here to let me express my true feelings so that I can be open and receptive to my sister telling me what to do, when to do it, how to do it, and giving me ridiculous reasons why I have to do it all, exactly as *she* says!"

Sam's interactions with women had been limited in the last two years. And though he was out of practice, Riley's torrent reminded him of similar conversations he'd had during his marriage. He'd all but forgotten the way women expressed their frustrations in long rages, their voices speeding up, their pitch escalating, putting it all out there in a way that men seldom did. He hadn't realized how much he missed such things until this moment, sitting in Riley's kitchen. He was struck silent by the feeling of déjà vu, not that Riley was ready for any input by him.

"I mean, I get it. This is her world. She knows how to play this game, and I don't. But it just seems to me that she could be a bit more humble about it. Why does she have to make everything a lesson?"

She stood then and made her way to the counter. Her question hung rhetorically in the air. He might be out of practice, but he was on his game enough to realize that she wasn't looking for him to answer it.

"I haven't managed to get to the grocery store this week, but I do have a nice bottle of Shiraz." She turned and reached for a bottle of wine that sat in a rack on top of the refrigerator. She faced him with a pleading smile.

"It really would be the exclamation point on this day if you made me drink alone."

"Oh, sorry, I didn't realize this was a question I was

supposed to answer." He couldn't help but tease her. Another thing he had lost about himself in the last few years was the lightness a bit of good-natured ribbing could bring to a conversation.

But in his defense, it was hard to tease when all anyone wanted to talk about was the saddest thing that had ever happened to you. Especially because the subtext of those conversations was their relief that he had lost a spouse instead of them. There wasn't much room for teasing when you were the perpetually grieving widower.

"In that case, I'll decide," Riley jibed good-naturedly back at him. "A glass of wine would be great for both of us."

She set the bottle down and began to rifle through a drawer. Not finding what she was looking for, she opened another, and then another. Finally, she found a corkscrew and began cutting the foil to open the bottle.

Sam considered helping her, but before he could even ask, she was setting down glasses and filling them with the deep red wine. They were the type that resembled juice glasses, like those he remembered from a trip to Italy. They suited her; they were not fancy and they served their purpose.

"The thing about Trish is, I never really gave much thought to what her life entailed. It was different than mine; I knew that. And a lot of it seemed sort of frivolous to me. I didn't get it. I think she's thrilled at the idea of showing me how important it all is. But the thing is, even though I'm knee-deep in this PTA hooey, I still don't get it."

It wasn't so much a rant as a confession. As she took a sip of her wine, the cast of vulnerability crossed her face again, and Sam was inclined to answer this time.

"Maybe it's not about showing you up, but hoping to earn the respect of her smart, successful sister?"

This was met with the usual eye roll.

"Trish, want my respect? Please, our whole lives have been about who was doing things the right way. She doesn't want my respect. She wants me to concede that all these years she was right and I was wrong. You'll see when she gets here. She lives and breathes this whole PTA thing—makes Cupcake and her crew look like novices."

"Maybe this whole thing goes deeper than the PTA and sibling rivalry." He knew his role here was as a sounding board, but, without conscious thought, he easily slipped into the role of devil's advocate that he had so often played with his late wife.

"Deeper how?"

"It seems as though you carry a bit of a chip on your shoulder when it comes to stay-at-home moms."

"Me? I think you have that backward. *They* have a chip on their shoulders toward any woman who chooses to work and have children. As though not devoting my entire life to mothering somehow makes me less of one."

He had hit a nerve, and though he risked adding to her

already stressful day, he pushed it. "Obviously it is a debate that has raged for years, but for you, I think you might be making assumptions that just aren't there."

"Come on Sam, you saw the way those women treated me at the very first meeting, and all of the ones since. They want to make sure I understand that I don't fit in because I work." Her exasperation was evident, but the spirit of the debate was not heated, just a mature exchange of ideas.

"I agree that they haven't been very welcoming, but, as you said, these are women who have devoted their entire lives to their children. Wouldn't they be protective of the school those kids go to?"

"Maybe, if they were sane," she said, attempting to lighten the mood. But he could tell by the tightening of her brow that he'd given her something to think about.

"I just wonder if you are chairing this event for Noah or to prove to them that your way is the right way."

He was looking at her intently as he said it, and without thinking he reached across the table and brushed away a curl that had fallen across her face. Realizing what he'd done, he quickly pulled his hand back, but it didn't seem to faze her.

She was quiet, as though she was really thinking about the question. Sam worried he'd pushed it too far, added to what had obviously been a stressful day and a subject that she struggled to understand herself. He was considering apologizing and telling her to forget the whole thing, but then she spoke.

"Honestly, at this point, I'm not sure what to think. I just want to feel like I am remotely capable of doing everything I'm supposed to for my son."

The look on her face brought him right back to wanting to pull her into his arms and offer her some comfort, but instead he took a drink of his wine and nodded. He was finding there was a great deal he wanted to say and learn where Riley Andrews was concerned, but first he had some things to straighten out with his son.

Chapter Thirteen

Traditionally, we number the centerpieces and raffle them off throughout the evening. That way you don't have to bother with favors or finding a way to dispose of the flowers."

Riley wondered how many times her sister had said "traditionally" in the last, she checked her watch, *four hours!*

She glanced at Sam, noting the dazed look on his face and the way he was flipping his pencil through his fingers, as though he was trying to either stay awake or keep from declaring the entire meeting an utter waste of time. The legal pad in front of him was completely blank. She glanced down at her own to find that, aside from a scribble or two, it was the same. In her entire life she had never sat through a meeting, class, or lecture of even a half hour's duration and not taken a single note.

To say the evening was pointless would be untrue. There were the moments of enlightenment that came from her earlier discussion with Sam. She'd taken his perspective into account throughout Trish's droning on and on about flower arrangements and invitations, having not once pointed out that those details were why there were committees, or that the success of the gala had more to do with the money raised than if the women thought she had picked a good color scheme. Who the heck cared if the glitter around the center-pieces matched the ribbon color on the balloons?

Trish cared, that's who. And she urgently wanted Riley to understand why *she* should care, so Riley shut up and listened to her sister. That small sign of respect did seem to be helping things along. There had been lit-tle to no condescension the entire night, no dramatic sighs, and Riley hadn't rolled her eyes once. So, if that was a measure of success, then the evening had been a smashing one.

And then there was the look on Daniel's face when he had dropped off Noah. The way he had sized Sam up and taken note of the friendly nature between Trish and Sam. Stared at him a bit too long, shook his hand a bit too firmly. All that man stuff that, despite herself, made Riley feel a rush of attraction to Sam. She man-aged to get hold of it by staring at the band of gold on Sam's left hand, something Daniel had failed to notice. So his ridiculous testosterone rush was her own private irony.

Now, with Noah tucked in bed, the clock inching ever closer to midnight, and Trish seeming to get to the end of her eleven-page outline for the meeting, Riley found a sense of giddy calm spreading through her. It had started with the glass of wine she and Sam had shared earlier but it was not because of it. The wine, the cashew chicken, and having an outline for what needed to be done for the gala had helped Riley's mood along significantly. Stealing a glance at Sam, she knew he was the main reason why she felt so in control.

It made no logical sense, and she knew it. How could a situation that had her head spinning and her heart racing make her feel content? After the day she had just experienced, she really wasn't in the frame of mind to question it. She was just going with it, though her eyes remained focused on the shiny band of gold.

"So that's all I have." If ever there was a time for an "Amen," that was it, and while she considered saying it out loud, Riley knew it would turn their pleasant unspoken truce on its ear. Instead, she flipped her outline closed, catching Sam's eye across the table.

Ever so slightly, he raised one eyebrow; his eyes seemed to twinkle a bit. It was as though they could communicate without words. This whole PTA situation had given them a common battleground, but only when it reached the level of being completely ridiculous. They had just spent more than four hours talking about a fundraiser, and the word *finance* hadn't been so much as whispered.

Dare she rock the boat and ask about the actual fundraising part of the gala?

"Trish, that is some great information, really helpful.

I'm wondering if we could touch on the items that are auctioned off, or the strategies the PTA has used in the past to raise a good amount of money at the event?"

It was as though she had spoken the words herself. Riley's mouth hung open as she stared at Sam, the deepness of his voice creating a tremor in the air of the dining room.

It was ridiculous how affected she was by his mere presence, let alone when he said something that made so much sense. There was not a great deal of common sense in her world at the moment.

She turned to look at Trish, knowing her sister would not like the inference that she had perhaps let something fall through the cracks. But instead of shooting daggers from her beautiful steel-blue eyes, she just gave a slight chuckle, similar to the one she gave Riley, but not quite as condescending.

"Sam, I can assure you that the donations and money will come in. The things I have presented to you tonight are what will make or break this event." She leaned forward, cocking her head to the side and smiling. "Trust me on this one. Your theme is the most important element of this event."

Riley shuddered. There was so much she wanted to say, starting with, "Is this the prom or a PTA fundraiser for our children's school?"

Theme?

To some degree she understood the concept; she was

in advertising, and packaging was important. She had to disagree, however, that it was the most important thing.

"Not that I don't trust you, but where *do* the items come from?" Riley made a concerted effort to keep her tone even, not giving a hint of how ridiculous she thought her sister's previous statement was.

To her amazement, Trish shrugged. "They just come. I have no idea from where or how."

"No idea? How is that possible?" Sam was as mystified as Riley.

"Again, you two are missing the point entirely."

As incredible as it was that her sister, having run this event for years, had no idea whatsoever where the items up for auction came from, it was equally as intriguing to Riley that Trish wasn't getting defensive as they questioned her. She was playing it a bit coyly, in fact. For a second it crossed Riley's mind that the whole thing was some sort of racket.

"No, I think we clearly understand the importance of the ambiance for the evening." Riley waved her copy of Trish's outline in the air to punctuate her point. "It's just that usually at a fundraiser billed as an auction there is a bit more attention paid to the items that will be used to make the money. How can they just appear? Do they just fall off a truck behind the gymnasium and you all just look the other way?"

Sam chuckled at this, and then added, "Or maybe you

meet some unshaven man in a Members Only jacket down near the river, some money changes hands, and then—*bada-bing*—you got yourself some auction items."

A smattering of laughter escaped from Trish's mouth, but the smile on her face seemed to get a bit tighter.

"This is what I know: the teachers send out the donation sheets, the donations appear, and the actual work for the event gets done." She stood and began packing up her things. "Regardless of what you two comedians think, the evening itself is what makes this a successful event as far as the members of the PTA are concerned."

She turned to Riley. "You two need to put your heads together, review my notes, and decide on a theme before we meet again. Now, will you walk me out?"

Riley was amazed. Trish wasn't mad or insulted. She wasn't throwing the usual fit. It was unnerving, as far as Riley was concerned, like when the creepy music escalates in a horror movie and you know someone is about to get an axe through the forehead.

And since she was walking her sister out, Riley was pretty sure she was about to get that axe.

"It was very nice to meet you, Sam. I look forward to working with you!" And Trish turned and swept out of the room, toward the front door.

Riley caught Sam's eye, his eyebrow once again raised, and she shrugged. She had no idea what had caused her sister's sudden departure. But as they reached the front step, Trish turned and was more than happy to drop her final bomb.

"I don't know what exactly is going on between you two, but you had best get a handle on your chemistry, or it isn't going to matter one bit what the theme is or if you break the donations record." She leaned forward, her tone and expression so dead serious that Riley nearly choked as she sucked her own "what the heck are you talking about" back inside her mouth.

"The only thing anyone will care or talk about is the fact that there is something going on between the co-chairs, one of whom is sporting a wedding band."

Trish nodded knowingly and then walked out the door, leaving Riley alone, stunned to hear put into words what she'd been thinking all night long.

Chapter Fourteen

Riley wrapped her fingers around the travel coffee mug. She held it tightly, as though the contents held the cure for cancer or something equally important, which to her it did. Sleep had not been her friend in the past week. She was wrestling with so many demons, and she had thus far managed to keep them all at bay by staying busy and avoiding any contact with Sam, Trish, or Daniel. Combine the constant flow of activity with the sleepless nights, and she was exhausted, thus the death grip on the coffee mug. Her other hand held just as tightly to the steering wheel of her car. The stress was getting to her.

She was making a concerted effort to ignore one resonating thought: maybe she wasn't cut out for this way of life. That perhaps she should concede, hire some help, and go back to work. But that felt too much like failure.

At least she had gotten some of the busywork for the auction done: the flier soliciting donations had gone out, and she had ordered the invitations, confirmed the location, and was waiting for a menu from the caterer. At any rate, she was actually doing something and not just having meetings about it. The event was, after all, a little over a month away. And she'd done all of it even though they hadn't picked a theme—Trish was horrified.

She was glad today she didn't have to deal with any of it. Glancing in the rearview mirror, she caught Noah's eye, and a smile spread across his face.

"Do you think they'll have those caramel apples with the chocolate chips on them?"

That smile was enough to make the day a success. Noah had been alternating between weepy and sassy the entire week. After the surprise pizza party with his father, they hadn't heard a word from him, and Noah was struggling. Riley knew it was probably time to get some sort of formal agreement in place with Daniel, for their son's sake. The thought of getting all those ducks in a row was overwhelming, however, and not something she cared to think about at the moment.

"I think they will have every kind of apple you can imagine at the Festival of Fall." She felt a little pull at her heart, glad to be doing something with Noah that would be an entire day for just the two of them—well, three, if the puppy counted. "I bet Ralph will help eat your leftovers." Without seeing him, Riley was certain that the puppy was curled up as close to Noah as he could possibly be, as he usually was when the child was still.

"Yeah, he probably would." His agreement was

peppered with small giggles, and Riley felt assured that this was exactly what they needed, just the crisp fall air and an entire day with nothing to do but enjoy themselves.

She had read about the festival in the paper that morning, and one look at the beautiful day breaking had cemented her decision. Not a cloud in the sky—you'd never know it had rained the entire night, except for the e-mail canceling all soccer games due to flooded fields, which was an answer to her prayers. The thought of spending the beautiful day dealing with any of the PTA moms who had kids on Noah's team, whether it be conversations about the auction, kiss-ups, or whispers, was not appealing to her in the least.

They exited the highway, as directed by the confident voice of the GPS Riley had rarely used. Soon they were passing the wide expanse of fields and farms cut by groves of trees, their leaves exploding in hues of gold and crimson. This was going to be a day they would both remember. That was even more important than her escape, Riley thought, as she saw the sign for the festival ahead and slowed to make the turn into the apple orchard.

She had barely put the car in park before Noah was unbuckling his seat belt and fumbling to get out of the car. Thankfully, he at least remembered to grab Ralph's leash before he opened the door, or the excited puppy would have taken off in a flash and they would have had to chase him down. Instead, the boy and puppy stood by the car, practically aquiver.

An inflatable moon bounce, as big as a house and in the shape of an apple, stood just inside the gate; a horse pulling a hayride cart pulled up beyond that. Signs pointed the way to a corn maze and listed the various food vendors, a pumpkin patch, and more.

"What should we do first?" Riley asked, grabbing her son by the hand and heading in the direction of a small wooden building where they could pay their entrance fee.

"We should probably start at the beginning and make our way through, so we don't miss anything!"

Noah's exclamation filled her with a rush of motherly love, not only because of its enthusiasm, but also because of his logic. It was exactly what she was planning to do. And so, after purchasing their tickets, they proceeded to the moon bounce, where Noah carefully removed his shoes, climbed through the opening, and began bouncing as high as his legs and boundless energy would allow. Riley wrapped the leash around her wrist, whipped out her camera, and began snapping what would be, she was sure, the first of many pictures. She wanted to remember this day.

Over the next few hours they meticulously and gleefully made their way around the festival. They picked apples, found their way through the maze, rode the hayride and the ponies, visited the petting zoo, and, after Noah got his face painted to resemble a scarecrow, found their way to the food section, both famished and ready to sit for a bit. Ralph, it seemed, was also ready for a rest. He was no longer pulling at his leash, but rather walking calmly beside her. Maybe this was the day the puppy would finally concede that she was in control. It was, after all, the first day in a long while that she felt as though she were.

"You having fun, buddy?" she asked as they wolfed down their hot dogs and curly fries and eyed the plate of steaming funnel cakes topped with warm cinnamon apples that awaited them when they finished.

"The best time! Can we ride on the Spinning Apples next?" He pointed over her shoulder to where six-foot-tall shiny red apples spun on sturdy green arms, lights twinkling everywhere. The thought of climbing inside a giant apple and spinning for five minutes made Riley a bit queasy, but saying no was out of the question.

"Of course we can."

"And get a caramel apple?"

"Maybe we should finish all this before we get something else to eat," she said, indicating the plates of food in front of them. Noah happily obliged, grabbing a handful of fries and cramming them in his mouth, careful not to smudge the yellow paint that covered his face.

"And maybe we should have gone on the Spinning Apples *before* we stuffed ourselves?"

"Oh, we'll be fine," he said, his voice full of an eight-year-old's confidence.

And sure enough, he was right. The taste of the delicious funnel cake still in her mouth, Riley climbed aboard and spun with her son, both of them erupting in giggles. After that, he won a stuffed bear bobbing for apples. Finally, after they had visited every game, ride, and activity, and Riley's arms were weighed down by the bag of apples they had picked in one hand and a gallon of cider in the other, they made their way to the car, Noah holding Ralph's leash in one hand and a divine-looking caramel apple in the other. It had been sliced by the vendor and put into a Styrofoam bowl to make it easier for him to eat, which she knew he would do the minute his seat belt was buckled.

It had been a good day, exactly what she had both hoped for and needed. As she pulled out of the apple farm, Riley felt for the first time in many days that she had a handle on her life. It was a refreshing turn of events. She glanced in the rearview mirror and could see Noah happily munching on his apple, licking the excess caramel from his fingers, an impatient whine coming from Ralph as he waited for his turn to lick.

"Try this," she said, pulling a wipe from her purse and handing it over her shoulder.

I really am a competent mother. I even carry Handi-wipes in my purse.

The thought brought a ridiculous smile to her face, but still, it was good to feel as though she was doing something right. Prior to diving into the full-time mom role, she had done quite a few things right, even taking care of Noah. She had somehow forgotten that, with all the other things swirling around her. She had been a successful working mom, and that success had not been limited to her work. She'd been pretty good at the mom part too.

It wasn't until they were nearing the exit to their house that the calm peace was shattered.

"Mom, I don't feel right."

"Like you're going to be sick?" Riley felt a surge of panic—vomit all over the car was not something even Handi-wipes would take care of.

"No, my throat is scratchy, and my tongue feels funny. And it's hard to breathe." His words were jumbled, as though he had marbles in his mouth, and a wheeze escaped from his mouth as he gasped for another breath. She glanced into the rearview mirror to see that his lips were puffy.

"It's okay, honey. We're almost home," she said, careful to keep her voice as normal as possible even as alarm surged through her. She scanned the shoulder of the road searching for an exit sign. There was a hospital a few exits before theirs, but she had no idea how many or if they had already passed it. She didn't know if she should speed up or slow down. Her eyes darted from the road to Noah's face in the rearview mirror, and then to her purse, which held her cell phone, and then repeated the pattern. Her heart pounded as a sense of panic started to swell there.

"Just keep talking to me, baby," she said, her voice as calm as she could make it. She could hear him wheezing as he breathed in the back.

In the distance, a green exit sign appeared, and she slowed as they approached it. Looking for a blue hospital sign and seeing none, she took a deep breath. Slowing her racing heart, she glanced again at her son's face, and suddenly, the panic ceased. There was no time for it; she had to take care of this. Glancing again for a road sign, her eyes fell on the GPS, and with relief, she punched the buttons that brought up the live map, and then turned on the search function and typed in "hospital." Within seconds the reassuring voice spit out the words she needed to hear.

"Destination, St. Francis Hospital, 1.7 miles ahead."

"It's going to be okay, baby. Just keep taking as deep of breaths as you can manage." She reached her hand back and patted his knee, his small hand wriggling into hers. She modeled the breathing loudly, willing him to do the same. He nodded and did his best to follow suit. Frightened tears filled his eyes, but they did not spill onto his red cheeks.

"Exit Elm Street .5 miles on the right."

Ahead the exit appeared like the salvation that it was, and she sped up as she merged onto the ramp. Now that she was off the highway, she knew how to get to the hospital, but the voice of the navigator was helping to keep her calm, so she listened as it guided her the rest of the way.

"Noah, sweetie, we're at the hospital." She glanced in the back. "Everything will be okay."

Slamming her car into park, she jumped from her

seat. She fumbled with her own door handle and then Noah's. Finally it opened, and she scooped him up in her arms and raced toward the emergency room, her newfound confidence and peace of mind both badly shaken by her worry for her son.

As she reached the sliding door, she caught the eye of a nurse. Within seconds, Noah was out of her arms and on a gurney, as Riley calmly explained the sequence of events that had brought them there.

"Sounds like an allergic reaction to something."

Riley looked up into the face of the doctor, his hair graying at the temples, his tone calm and reassuring. She gave thanks for his age and wisdom. His orders to the nurses who were methodically buzzing around Noah were swift, and then he turned to speak directly to her.

"We're giving him a shot of adrenaline to stop the reaction. Once his breathing is normal, we'll do some testing and figure out what the reaction was to."

Riley nodded, her eyes focused on Noah and what she hoped was a calming smile on her face, his small hand in hers. Her son did not even notice as the nurse stuck his arm with the shot; only by reflex did he squeeze her fingers. And then, within seconds, his breathing seemed to ease and return to normal. Still, she did not completely relax. Only when the nurse patted her arm did she feel like she could breathe again.

"Good job, Mom," the kind young woman said. "You got him here. He's going to be just fine."

And with that, Riley was filled with a pride that eclipsed anything she had ever done professionally. She was competent at this, more than competent. And she carried Handi-wipes too.

Chapter Fifteen

T hough her actual calm did not last long, Riley could still feel the warmth of having handled the crisis so smoothly. Noah was breathing normally, but the doctor wanted to keep him for observation since his reaction had been so severe. They were also waiting for the results of the tests that would tell them just what he was allergic to, and for a room on the pediatric ward to be assigned to Noah.

Riley had pushed for the test, insisting that she needed to at least be aware of what to avoid, even if an allergist could give her a more thorough report. Chalk another one up for the mom who had a handle on the crisis.

Now she had another, albeit less critical, crisis to resolve. Ralph. The puppy had behaved well in the first two hours he had been left in the car unattended, but that couldn't continue, not if she didn't want her car chewed up, or worse. She had pretty much decided that calling Trish would be more trouble than help—she didn't need her sister telling her what to do when she had Noah's medical crisis well in hand. She had already left a message for Daniel, calmly explaining where they were and what had happened, and assuring the recording that their son was fine.

Really, in her current world, the only one left to help her, by taking care of Ralph, was Sam. He would help, she knew, without question.

Her son was in the hospital, she couldn't leave, and her puppy was in the car. It made logical sense, but she still hesitated. Not because she thought he would say no, but because she had managed to avoid Sam the entire week, and in doing so had managed to avoid thinking about how accurate Trish's observation was. There was definite chemistry between them. Riley couldn't deny or ignore it, so, instead, she managed to avoid Sam all together. But now she was in a bind, and she needed him.

Maybe the mystery wife could come and pick up Ralph?

Riley was prone to internal sarcastic dialogue when she was nervous or unsettled. As unproductive as it was, at least it kept her from insulting people. And it went along with her mantra.

A nurse arrived in their ER cubicle with a tray of food that Riley could see included both Jell-O and chocolate pudding, a clear indication that Noah would be entertained for a bit. With that and the all-too-familiar sound of his favorite cartoon on the TV opposite him, he would be well occupied.

"Noah, I need to step outside and make a quick call, okay?"

He nodded at her and then turned his attention to the tray of food in front of him. "Can I eat the pudding first?"

"Well, I don't see why not. You go ahead, Mom, we've got this under control." It was the nurse who had been so kind when they first arrived. Riley hadn't recognized her face, but her sweet voice was imprinted in Riley's memory.

She smiled at the woman's continuing kindness and, knowing that Noah was in such caring hands, slipped out of the room, out the revolving door, and into the night air. She had a weird sense of lost time, like when you go to a matinee and then find that night has come while you were in the darkened theater. Somehow it feels as though an entire day has been lost when all that was missed was the sunset.

Riley was also suddenly aware of how tired she was. Physically and emotionally, she was drained from the events of the day. It just didn't seem possible that it was the same Saturday.

She sat down on the concrete bench, fished out her phone, and punched in Sam's number before she had any more time to think about it.

He answered on the third ring. "Hello?"

"Hey, Sam. It's Riley. I need some help."

"Centerpieces, or sounding board?" he asked, and she could almost see his eyes light up as he ribbed her.

"Oh, I wish it was something as mundane as that. I'm at the hospital."

"Are you and Noah all right?" His tone changed instantly to one of concern.

"Yes, we're fine now. Noah had an allergic reaction to something. We aren't sure what, and they are keeping him overnight for observation. The problem is Ralph. He was with us when Noah had the reaction, and now he's stuck in my car."

"Which hospital? I'll be right there."

Riley could feel the relief spread through her. He would help, and she hadn't even had to ask.

"St. Francis, on Highland," she said, and then, "Sam, thank you."

"No thanks needed. I'll be right over."

As she hung up the phone, a smile spread across her face. The sort of smile that felt intensely private, though obviously there for the whole world to see. And for the moment, she didn't try to hide the fact that seeing Sam pleased her. Or to talk herself out of it. But then she was struck by the thought that maybe these feelings for Sam were really just about him being so dependable. Once again he was there, supporting her when she needed him. It had nothing whatsoever to do with lust or longing; it was just the overwhelming relief that someone was in her corner.

This awareness flooded her with relief. She wasn't in love with a married man. She had formed a friendship with an honest, supportive, trustworthy person who just happened to be male. It all made so much sense. Now that she was feeling competent, she could see the situation with some clarity.

Her smile broadened, and she continued to rationalize their relationship all the way back to Noah's cubicle in the ER, where her son had finished his dinner and was excitedly flipping the channels on his own personal television. Joy at seeing him well again replaced all thoughts of Sam, and Riley wondered how long that would go on. Would seeing him breathing normally fill her with such comfort forever, or just for the near future? She really didn't care if it was ridiculous to be so pleased with something so small. It brought her a sense of comfort, and that was all she cared about.

"Good dinner, buddy?" she said, brushing his cheek with her fingers.

"The nurse went to get me some more pudding," he said, smiling at her, but then quickly refocusing his attention back on the television.

Riley turned and sat down in the chair next to his bed. Together they watched cartoons, Riley taking pleasure in Noah's smiles and giggles as the colorful characters chased one another and fought on the screen.

A light tap on the door interrupted the peace she was feeling, and before she could say "come in" the door opened and the doctor entered.

"Mrs. Andrews, I have the preliminary results from the allergy screening," he said, flipping through a chart, not looking up. Riley stood up and met him at the side of Noah's bed.

Though she knew it was a bit over-the-top to feel such a sense of pride, Riley found she couldn't help it. It had been such a long time since she felt as though she was doing something right. Her shining moment was at once brought into perspective when the doctor met her eye.

"Your son has a very serious peanut allergy. This kind of thing can be life threatening, and you need to be vigilant about what he eats, even what his playmates eat."

Life threatening. Those two words were all it took to knock her swelling pride right out of her. Noah could have died. Riley suddenly felt nauseous and unsteady on her feet.

She swayed, but was caught as a hand reached out and wrapped around her waist, pulling her close.

"It's going to be okay. You got him here. He's out of danger now."

She knew without looking that it was Sam. Knew by the sound of his voice and the relief she felt that he was there.

"Could this have been his first reaction?" Sam asked, and his calm, inquiring voice centered Riley. She felt her nerves soothe and her focus return.

"It's hard to say." The doctor looked up, taking note of the new person in the room. "At some point he may have presented with a rash around his mouth, or a bit of raspy breathing that cleared on its own, but nothing this critical. Are you Noah's father?"

"He most certainly is not," came yet another voice, and Riley turned to see that Daniel, red-faced and breathing as though he'd run a marathon, had appeared in the room.

He crossed the small area from the door to the bed and put his hand on Noah's small chest. The boy's face lit up at the appearance of his father.

"Daddy!"

"How you feeling, buddy?" Daniel asked, his voice noticeably more tender than it had been when he'd arrived. He settled down on the bed next to Noah, pulling the boy into his arms.

"Great. I had the best day with Mommy, and now I'm having pudding for dinner, so all in all a pretty super day!"

"That's great."

"I'm Noah's father, Daniel Andrews. How did this happen?"

"I was just telling your wife"—the doctor paused, seeming to take note of Sam's arm around Riley's waist—"er, Noah's mother, that a peanut allergy is tricky. It can cause a serious reaction the very first time. Now that we are aware of it, you can take precautions." The beeper on his hip sounded, and he pulled it out and looked at it. "I've got to run. I know you have other questions, so I'll stop back. Sorry, the ER has been crazy tonight."

As the doctor left the room, Riley was suddenly aware

of Sam's embrace. She stepped slightly away from him before turning to tell him what she needed.

As if he read her mind, he spoke first.

"Riley, where's your car? I'll go and rescue Ralph. I was planning on my house, if you don't mind. That way you won't have to worry about getting home to take care of him."

Riley fished in her purse and pulled out her keys. "It's in the emergency parking lot. I'm sure you will hear him barking. Thanks, Sam." She met his eye, hoping her newfound peace with their friendship would translate in her glance. But instead, the quickening of her pulse returned.

"Okay. Noah, you take care, and keep up the pudding orders. This place has a never-ending supply." He winked at the boy, ignoring Daniel's glare, as he turned and left the room.

"Sam's nice," Noah said almost as an afterthought as he turned his attention back to the television. Riley found herself quietly agreeing with her son, and she was very aware of the warmth she still felt on her back where his arm had been just moments earlier.

Daniel stood, leaning in to whisper in Riley's ear, "Yeah, if you like deceitful manipulators."

"What are you talking about?" Riley shot back, her own whisper a bit more intense. She turned and walked out of the room motioning for Daniel to follow her. She didn't really have the energy to fight with the man, but she certainly didn't want to do it in front of Noah.

Stepping into the hall, his face full of excitement over the news he was about to deliver, he said, "I made some calls. The admissions secretary at Hubbard always did have a bit of a crush on me. Seems your new 'friend' isn't being entirely honest. Portrays himself as this family man, but the truth of the matter is, there is no wife listed on that kid's registration forms. Makes you wonder, doesn't it? Why's he lying about it? What does he have to hide?"

Riley felt as though she'd been punched in the stomach. And while the delivery was meant to hurt her, the news did nothing but knock her off balance. Sam was single, no wife. Her feelings for him weren't wrong.

But he had lied to her. Dependable Sam, who kept her from spinning out of control, had been lying to her from the start.

Chapter Sixteen

As Sam stood in his backyard, Ralph running from tree to bush to fence, he wondered why he hadn't heard from the puppy's owner. Obviously, her plate was full—having met both Riley's sister and her husband, he had a new understanding about why she tended to be a bit high-strung. And clearly, she had Noah to worry about and take care of, but still, he hadn't heard a word since he'd returned her keys the night before. She'd seemed strange even then. Looked at him with such a vacant stare, as though she hardly knew who he was. He could tell something was off. And while he'd dismissed it because of the situation, now he was downright worried.

Watching the dog run in circles, Sam couldn't help but think he'd been doing the same thing for the past few weeks. Doing all he could to avoid the obvious. His attraction to Riley had developed into something decidedly more important in his life. And though she was a bit neurotic and brought some baggage, the rush he got at just the sight of her the night before could not be ignored.

He also knew that Max was not as big of a problem as he had made him out to be. His son was adjusting nicely to their new town and his new school. He had loads of friends—the best of whom was Noah. There was no doubt in Sam's mind that his son was more than ready for everyone to know the truth about his mom. It would probably be a relief to share what a wonderful woman she had been, instead of living with the mystery she had become.

The bigger difficulty was accepting the fact that Sam himself had developed real feelings for another woman, and that it was okay. It wasn't disloyal to the memory of Maggie. She would be thrilled with the prospect of him finding some happiness outside of fatherhood. But the guilt of it remained, and he knew that was a bigger factor in not letting Riley know he was a widower. Telling her would remove the obstacle between them, one he had put there himself. And once it was gone, there would be no turning back. It was terrifying and thrilling at the same time.

It was amazing to Sam that he could have serious feelings for a woman again. He was so sure after Maggie died that his life would be just about Max. Anything more seemed out of the question. But he knew this wasn't about seeking out a new woman in his life; it was about Riley. She was the reason the part of him that had shut down when his wife died had appeared again.

"Ralph! Ralph! Come here, boy!" With the energy only a child could possess at the end of the day, Max suddenly appeared from the back door and ran past Sam, calling for the dog he had fallen head over heels for in the twenty-four hours the pup had lived with them.

Taking note of the broad smile on Max's face, the pure joy in his voice, Sam thought maybe it was time they got a dog of their own. A Lab, probably black, but he wasn't opposed to a yellow one.

He sat down on the lawn furniture to watch the two of them play. Max pulled an old tennis ball from his pocket and threw it, Ralph racing after it. The perfect game of fetch, except that the dog wasn't quick to give the ball back, leaving Max to chase after him. When caught, Ralph would shower the boy's face in licks. But that seemed to be just an extension of the game, as Max giggled uncontrollably until Ralph finally released the ball and the whole thing began again.

Sam pulled the zipper on his sweatshirt to the top against the sudden chill in the air that accompanied the setting sun. He thought he should probably make Max put on a sweater of his own, but he didn't want to inter- rupt his fun. He knew that eventually one of them would tire of the game and they would all go in from the chilly fall evening.

Sure enough, twenty minutes later, the puppy had tired of fetch and collapsed in a heap at Sam's feet. Ralph gnawed at the ball for a few seconds before giving a big sigh and falling instantly asleep. Max climbed into his father's lap and snuggled in, his skin cold as he tucked his head under Sam's chin.

"What would you think about us getting a puppy?" Sam asked, and the answer was as quick as it was enthusiastic.

"When?" Max sat straight up, all snuggling forgotten. "Tomorrow?"

"I was thinking more along the lines of sometime in the next month," Sam said, laughing. "But when we do, you'll have to help me take care of it."

"No problemo, Daddy-o. I'll do whatever it takes."

Sam laughed that the boy who was still young enough to climb into his father's lap would be old enough to quip such slang.

"Buddy, I wanted to talk to you about something else."

"What?"

"Well, we've been here for a while now. And you've settled into school and soccer and made some friends. I'm thinking it's probably time to start telling the people close to us about your mom." He said it as lightly as he could, hoping not to disrupt the peace of the moment. It needed to be done, but Sam knew if Max was upset it would be hard for him to press the issue.

In his lap the boy sighed and pushed closer to his chest. "You're right. Some of my friends at school have been asking me about Mom, and I didn't know what to say. It seems wrong to not tell the truth, like we're ashamed of her, when we aren't." He turned bright pricks of tears in his green eyes, his mother's eyes. "She was the best mom ever."

Sam swallowed hard, his own eyes feeling the sting of tears that were forming there. "You're right about that. She was. It would be nice to be able to talk about her and tell people how much we loved her."

"Do you think people are going to think different about me 'cause I don't have a mom?"

"Not the ones who matter, buddy."

"I think I'm going to start with Noah when he gets out of the hospital. When's that going to be anyway?"

"Probably tonight or tomorrow, but he'll rest a bit before we see him. How about we tell him and Riley when they come to pick up Ralph?"

At the sound of his name, the puppy stood up, tail wagging, and headed toward the back door.

"It must be time to feed him again." Max scrambled off Sam's lap and tugged hard on the door, tripping over the puppy as they made their way inside.

Sam sat for a second wrestling with his feelings, finding he was both relieved and apprehensive. Telling Riley about Maggie was not the hardest part; once it was done, there was nothing stopping him from telling her how he felt about her. For the first time he wondered how she would receive the news. While it was more than obvious she enjoyed his company, he wasn't sure what she would think of his being so attracted to her.

She was a bit overwhelmed at the moment, and knowing Riley as he did, her first reaction would be an overreaction. But he was getting used to those.

That decided, he stood to join his son inside, but a sudden buzz from the phone on his hip stopped him. When he glanced at the display, a fleeting hope that it might finally be Riley was cut short. It was a work call, and it coming this late on a weekend could only mean there was a problem.

Thirty minutes later, he hung up the phone. A crisis with a building he was designing needed his immediate attention. A quick call to his sister and another to the airlines, and he was ready to explain it all to Max.

"Hey, buddy, something's come up with one of my projects and I need to fly out first thing in the morning to fix it," he said, walking into the family room where Max was watching television. "But the good news is Aunt Aubrey is going to come out and take care of you until I can get back."

"But when will that be?" Sam was surprised by the angst in his son's voice.

Max adored his aunt—she was single, in her twenties, loved her nephew fiercely, and spoiled him endlessly. Max usually begged for Sam to stay away longer when Aubrey was his caretaker.

"I'm not sure yet. Why?"

Max, sitting curled up on the coach with Ralph, rubbed the puppy's ears. "Our puppy, remember?"

"Ah, yes," Sam said, relieved that the talk of Maggie

earlier had not caused the anguish. "We'll get the puppy as soon as I get back from Brazil."

"Brazil, huh? Aunt Aubrey's going to be here for at least a week. I'm thinking new Lego sets and ice cream for dinner."

He flashed an innocent smile and wiggled his eyebrows, and Sam could only laugh, because he knew that was exactly what would happen with his sister in charge. But they would both enjoy themselves, and Sam never had to worry about Max missing him when Aubrey was in charge.

He was just about to remind his son not to push his luck when the doorbell rang. Sam looked at his watch. "Who could that be at this hour?"

Walking to the door, he nearly tripped over Ralph who rushed in the same direction, and it dawned on Sam that it could very well be Riley coming to collect her puppy, and unload about the craziness of her life. The image of her twisting her hair around her finger as she vented at a rapid-fire pace made him almost run to open the door, heart racing.

But when he swung the door open he was left feeling like a foolish teenager. It wasn't Riley standing there, but Trish, who looked about as flustered as Sam felt.

"I'm here to get the puppy," she said, her tone all business, as she walked past him and into the house.

"It's nice to see you again, Trish. Where's Riley?" he asked, noting that her overly friendly, kiss-up demeanor was gone.

"She's getting Noah settled at home and asked me to come here."

No doubt about it, with her clipped words and failure to meet his eye, something was definitely wrong. And her behavior was faintly reminiscent of Riley's last night, like he'd done something horrible.

"Is everything okay? Noah?"

"It's fine. He's fine," she replied coolly. Perplexed, Sam was about to press further, but he was stopped by the puppy, who began whining. This brought Max running to see what all the commotion was about.

"Do you have a leash or something?"

"Yeah, we actually went a bit overboard buying things to make him happy. Let me bag it all up so you can give it to Riley," Sam said, stepping past her.

Trish scooped up the puppy, his fur immediately clinging to her designer suit.

"No time for that. I'm sure Riley has everything she needs." She leaned in close, finally looking him square in the eye. "My sister has always been able to take care of herself."

Then she turned, walked out the still-open front door, calling back over her shoulder. "I'm sure she'd want me to thank you for watching the dog, so thanks." And then she was gone, walking briskly into the dark, struggling to keep the wiggling puppy in her arms.

"Why'd she go so fast with Ralph and leave all the stuff we bought him?" Max asked, closing the door behind her grand exit.

"I have no idea," Sam replied, shaking his head.

But I know enough to know it was about something.

Sam also knew that whatever it was, Trish would only add to the drama. But he had no time to deal with it until he returned from his trip, which now seemed extremely ill timed.

Chapter Seventeen

It had been two days, and Riley was resolute that she had enough on her plate and would not allow this wrinkle with Sam to trip her up. She had somehow convinced Trish to pick up Ralph without much explanation, and thus far she had managed to avoid the topic of Sam altogether. But Trish was intuitive enough to know there was something going on. She'd made that clear when she dropped off the dog.

"I told him you didn't need any more help," she'd proclaimed proudly, leaving Riley to wonder if perhaps Daniel had clued Trish in on Sam's marital situation.

After getting Noah home, she had called the school to make sure the nurse and his teacher were trained to administer Noah's epi-pen. She'd called the allergist to schedule a follow-up appointment, even made sure to coordinate with Daniel's schedule so he could be there too. As worried as she was about Noah, she was thankful for the purpose it gave her. It was like coordinating a big project at work—making sure all the details were covered. And she was applying the same mindset to the gala.

This was *her* project; she was in charge of it, and that was how she was proceeding. No more hiding behind her sister or depending on Sam. She was doing it on her terms, starting with the location for today's planning meeting. Instead of the school library or the coffee-house, she had reserved a conference room at the public library. It gave her a boost of confidence that she wasn't walking onto anyone's turf. It was an even playing field, except for the fact that she was in charge.

She checked the clock on her dashboard, pleased to see she was thirty minutes early, as she pulled into the library parking lot. It gave her plenty of time to set up the room before the others arrived. She had dressed in her least imposing business suit, which she hoped would emphasize her new resolve.

She was prepared, confident, and in control. The old Riley wasn't just back—she was better than ever, and applying the things she was good at to the life she was leading. What could possibly go wrong?

She parked the car and quickly gathered the materials she needed from the backseat, including copies of the agenda, fresh donuts, and a bag of whole-grain, organic muffins.

The muffins were for her own personal enjoyment—given the temptation, she wanted to see how many of those size zeros would choose a muffin that tasted like sawdust over a delightful, still-warm donut. She'd brought coffee too, although she knew most of the women would probably bring their own lattes or cappuccinos or spiced-chai-tea-whatevers. She knew Sam would have gotten the joke, but she couldn't spend any more time thinking about him.

As if on cue, her cell phone rang and she glanced down to see Sam's number.

He's been lying to you. Remember? The only reason to take this call is because of the gala.

Nothing more.

Now who's the one lying?

Finding her internal debate too much to sort through in the amount of time that she had, Riley sent his call to voice mail. She inhaled deeply, trying to exorcise the feelings that Sam brought up. There was no place for them at the moment, but Riley was well aware from the number of times he'd called that she was going to have to deal with him eventually.

Juggling the bags and boxes, her briefcase, and her keys, she climbed out of her car.

"Do you need a hand?"

Surprised, Riley looked up into the kind face of a woman she didn't recognize. "Thanks, but I've got it," she replied as the top box, holding the agendas, slipped from the pile and fell to the pavement. And before Riley could readjust her load, the woman bent down and scooped them all up.

Working to straighten the pile, she glanced at the

sheet in her hand, and then up at Riley, her kind face now absolutely beaming.

"I'm Annie, former PTA slacker. When I heard someone from out of the ranks was chairing the gala, I had to come out and support you." Her tone rang of mockery with a hint of sarcasm. Riley liked her immediately.

"Well, I think you and I are going to get along just fine." She extended her hand. "Riley Andrews."

"Nice to meet you in person, though I've heard your name whispered in the halls and behind the stacks in the library." She winked. "Your legend precedes you."

Riley laughed. Legend? Most mornings she was lucky if she and Noah got out the door in clean clothes with any sort of breakfast eaten.

"I'm no legend," she scoffed as they reached the door of the library.

"Seriously, the way you took Stephanie Ann to task, wrenching this event from her hands and planning it without consulting any of the queen bees?" Annie pulled the door open and waited for Riley to walk through. "You're a legend to me and my kind."

The conversation was interrupted by the woman at the help desk. After checking them in, she gave strict instructions about the meeting room's location and the need for it to be left as clean as it was found. They wound their way through the corridors to the elevator. Taking that up one floor, they crossed the small hall into an immaculate meeting room. Riley quickly began setting it up to her liking, all the while mulling over what Annie had said to her. Was there some sort of underground network of moms who supported the school without sitting through PTA meetings? The thought had never occurred to her.

"So, why don't you tell me about your slacker nation?" Riley said when the chairs had been placed around the table, an agenda placed at each seat.

"We're a pretty regular group of women, trying to support the school but not interested in playing politics or kissing butts," Annie said matter-of-factly, and Riley smiled, liking the woman more and more.

"So, you don't work?"

"Oh, I work, just not at anything I get paid for." Her reply did not take on the defensive tone Trish's always did when the subject came up.

"I never thought of it that way," Riley said, thoughtfully. "You're right, staying home, taking care of my son, and trying to get all this right is more work than when I actually went to my job."

Annie smiled. "Not to mention the whole declaring civil war on the ranking heads of the PTA. When this thing is all over, either you'll have won freedom for the rest of us, or you can come join me in the library, quietly reshelving books, far from the reach of the PTA posse!"

"Nice to know there are options if this thing is a bust."

"Oh, it won't be a bust. Not if I can help it." Annie glanced up. "We've got incoming."

Riley followed her gaze to see that the entire clan from the coffeehouse was making their grand entrance. Each of them was holding a very tall cup of coffee and was dressed to the nines in a variety of designer jeans and sweaters. Perfect hair, perfect makeup, perfect nails—they probably all had perfect pitch too. But for the first time their appearance as a group didn't rattle her. This was *her* meeting, *her* turf. That they had to arrive together actually made her feel a bit better. That and her new sidekick, Annie.

Glancing down at the agenda in front of her, Riley had an idea. She whispered in Annie's ear, and a smile spread across both of their faces.

"That's brilliant!" Annie sat down at the head of the table and began her assigned duty as Riley made her way to the approaching gaggle to greet them.

"Good morning, ladies!" she said, in a cheery yet professional tone, nothing like the howler-monkey greeting that usually began one of these meetings.

They all paused for a second, and Riley swore they blinked as though they couldn't understand her. She stood there and smiled, waiting for some sort of greeting or acknowledgement.

"All right. Well, I see you have coffee. I brought some snacks. Help yourselves." She pointed to the table on her left. "And since it would appear that everyone has arrived together, why doesn't everyone grab a seat and

let's get started. I'm sure we all have very busy sched-
ules today."

Finally, Cupcake spoke up, still obviously doing her
best to toe the line of loyalty to Stephanie Ann, but in
fear of crossing Trish. "This is a very important event,
and speaking for myself, I have blocked off my entire
morning to attend this meeting."

Riley smiled sweetly. "Well, luckily for you, you are
looking at some free time, because this is certainly not
going to take all morning." And with that she turned
and found her own seat, next to Annie, who had completed her task and was smiling with satisfaction.

The din of chatter rose as the women gathered by the
food table. Splitting the muffins in half to share them,
while the donuts box sat with the lid still firmly in place,
they seemed to be making no effort whatsoever to find
their seats.

They were bound and determined to turn her meeting
into a social gathering. Perhaps she shouldn't have
brought the food?

"Ladies," she called in a voice a bit louder than her
usual.

Nothing.

"Ladies!"

A bit louder now. Still no response.

Then from beside her, a whistle the likes of which she
hadn't heard since second grade cut the room. Annie,
her fingers still in her mouth, smiled up at her mischievously. The group at the buffet was finally shocked into

silence. From the looks on their faces, these women were not accustomed to being whistled to a halt.

"If you could all find your seats," Riley said, stifling her giggle as her former adversaries, too dazed to put up a fight, floated to the chairs and situated themselves around the table.

Riley herself sat down next to Annie. Leaning in, she whispered in her ear, "Thanks for getting their attention."

Annie nodded. "Look at how they save seats and must sit by their friends. It's like junior high all over again."

"Junior high on steroids, perhaps," Riley whispered, and then she turned up her volume. "In the interest of saving time, I have broken down this event into subcategories according to what needs to be done. I've assigned each of you a specific job. You take care of what you are assigned and report to me when it is done. If everyone does what they are supposed to do, this whole thing should go off without a hitch."

General whispering followed. It was the sort of white noise whose source is hard to detect. In a split second, the calm, placid faces erupted into disbelief, and the diluted whispers rose to all-out shouting. Riley glanced at Annie, who was leaning back in her chair, arms crossed, taking in the scene as if she were spending the morning at the zoo.

And then equally as shocking was the sudden silence as Stephanie Ann rose to speak. "I know you are new to this. However, in the past, we found that subcommittees are usually the best way to put this event together."

Riley stood herself, wondering why, but feeling the need to not let the woman look down on her. This was, after all, her meeting, and her way of doing things.

"I understand. But I thought that maybe this year we could forego the subcommittees, and additional meetings, and instead have everyone contribute in the area that is best suited for them."

Riley glanced around the room, and to her surprise, it appeared there were at least some receptive faces around the table. Quickly, she read down her list of tasks, and the woman assigned to them. She had planned on letting them sign up themselves, until Annie showed up. Annie was savvy and had been around the PTA block a few times. Having her assign the jobs was a stroke of brilliance.

As she read from the list, she glanced up and was satisfied to find that some of the women even looked pleased at this new arrangement, Cupcake and Screamer, who had been assigned to decorations, among them.

"So, does anyone have an objection to their assignment?"

Silence.

Riley held her breath, waiting for the chaos to erupt.

But instead, one lone voice posed a question. "So we take care of our assignment, and then report back to you for your approval?"

"No, not for my approval of anything, just completion," Riley replied, feeling as though she was explaining something that should go without saying. But from the looks on their faces, it had been a long time since this group had done anything without a committee.

Chapter Eighteen

At first Riley couldn't put her finger on what was so strange as she sat on her couch, the room lit only by the lamp beside her. Then it struck her—the silence. Her day had been filled with so much noise and activity that peace seemed out of place.

The gala meeting had started as chaos, but it had climaxed and finished with nervous chatter. As unbelievable as it was to her, the cronies of the PTA seemed almost in awe at her new procedure.

It was as if they had forgotten how to do anything on their own, or without someone telling them exactly what to do and how to do it. Annie said that Riley may have planted the seeds for revolution in the months to come, "if this thing is even remotely organized and successful."

She'd said it as they sat at lunch, celebrating the coup and the look on Stephanie Ann's face as, one by one, the women took their assignments, energized to accomplish their tasks. The most rewarding had been Cupcake and Screamer, who were thrilled at the idea that they could design the decorations and plan the theme all without having to gain approval from anyone. Oh, they had to coordinate with each other, but they were fine with that—more meetings at the coffeehouse to make sure everything matched the theme.

But they answered to no one. That was beyond their wildest dreams, as far as Riley could tell.

"You know, we were most worried that someone with no experience in planning this sort of event would screw the whole thing up with a bad theme," Cupcake had confided in her, unable to contain her pleasure. It was oddly similar to those beauty pageant moments that Riley had always believed were staged but that were apparently quite sincere.

But lunch and her insta-bond with Annie had been the highlight of the day. After months of hiding, fighting, and listening to only her sister, she'd found a like-minded person. Annie was smart and funny, and shed a new kind of light on the stay-at-home philosophy. She stayed home so that she could be the main influence in her kids' lives and be a hands-on mom. She was exactly what Riley needed as she ventured into this new phase of her life. Their lunch had stretched into the afternoon, and it would have lasted even longer if they hadn't had to pick up their kids.

"Thank you so much for coming out of the shadows to my meeting," Riley had said as they left the restaurant.

"Are you kidding me? You're like the Sally Fields of the PTA, and not the Flying Nun Sally, but the Norma Rae Sally. The one with the sign, except instead of it saying 'Union,' yours said 'Sanity.' "

Riley laughed. "Time will tell. I still have to pull the whole thing off before my revolution can be considered a success. And based on the sneer on Stephanie Ann's face, I wouldn't put her above sabotage."

"I'll keep my ear to the ground and let you know if I hear of any plots!"

They'd laughed, because most likely a plot would be hatched. Then Riley had a stroke of genius.

"Listen, Sam was supposed to be my co-chair, but he had to go out of town. Any interest in coming on board?"

"Be a part of this historic overthrow? Absolutely!"

Riley had been so relieved—she'd have help and she could put a bit of distance between herself and Sam. She knew eventually she would have to sort through her anger at him. But for the moment, just having him out of the picture would do.

After their long lunch, she'd picked Noah up from school, helped with his homework, and packed him up for his first overnight with his father. Who had managed to show up and not pick a fight with her about anything. In fact, the entire exchange had gone so smoothly that Riley had almost convinced herself that the ugly incident at the hospital the week before had been a fluke. Or maybe she was just in a better frame of mind because she'd had such a good day. Either suited her just fine.

So here she sat—her house quiet and dark, her demons at bay—not quite knowing what to do with herself. For the first time in months, she really felt like she and Noah were going to be all right. It called for some sort of commemoration, even if it was small and private. A personal victory called for a personal celebration. For Riley, that meant double-stuffed Oreos and milk in the family room, not at the kitchen table where she had to eat in order to set a good example for Noah.

Making her way to the kitchen, she made quick work of pouring the milk in a glass that was wide enough at the top for dunking. She grabbed the cookies from the cupboard and returned to the couch, grabbing her cell phone along the way. It would be better to have it if Noah called than to have to race around and find it when it rang.

I really am firing on all cylinders.

Settling in with her cookies and milk, she flipped the phone open to make sure the battery didn't need charging. Looking at the small screen, Riley's breath caught. She had forgotten that Sam had tried to call her earlier in the day. But there it was—one missed call, and a new voice mail. In the week since she had found out he was single and she had been avoiding his calls, he hadn't left a message. Despite her anger, she couldn't help but be intrigued.

He must need help with Max, she reasoned, trying to ignore the new race in her pulse. Deliberately, she punched the numbers that would play the voice mail, hoping the sound of his voice wouldn't cause the palpitations to increase.

"Riley, it's Sam. I'm not sure what's going on with you. You certainly seem to be avoiding my calls. I really need to talk to you about something pretty important. I'd ask you to call me back, but with the time change, that probably isn't going to work. You know, as much as I hate to do this, I'm just going to send you an e-mail. I hope nothing gets lost to interpretation." He laughed at that. The slight, warm chuckle, she knew, meant he was thinking seriously about what to say next. He'd done it every time they'd talked about anything remotely serious.

"I just hope you'll respond one way or another when you read it. Hope Noah is doing well. Max said he's been at school. I look forward to hearing from you soon." And then he was gone.

He had something to tell her. There was an e-mail. He hoped she would reply. Just moments earlier, she'd had such a handle on things, and now, well, now she was almost hyperventilating.

The message had been left that morning when she was going into the meeting, which should mean the e-mail would already be in her inbox. She dunked a cookie into her milk and took a bite.

But it was useless to even try to pretend she wasn't interested in what he had to say. And, as clichéd as it was, she couldn't ignore how the familiar sound of his voice had made her feel all tingly inside. She popped the rest of the cookie in her mouth and went to find her laptop. Might as well just read it instead of speculating on what it may or may not say.

She found her computer, sitting open and running on the desk in her kitchen. Leaning over it to pull up her e-mail, her hands quivered on the keyboard.

"For the love of Pete, get ahold of yourself," she muttered, knowing it was easier said than done. Her body was having a reaction to Sam that had nothing to do with her mind. Hoping to calm a bit of her nervous energy, she picked up the computer and walked briskly back to the couch and the cookies while the application launched. Not until she'd polished off two more did she glance again at the screen and see that there was, in fact, an e-mail from Sam, marked as urgent. The subject line read *Please don't ignore this, Riley.*

It's just an e-mail, Riley thought. *You've read hundreds of them.*

She moved her finger around the mouse pad and clicked on Sam's message. She took a deep breath, closed her eyes, popped an entire Oreo in her mouth, chewed, swallowed, and then opened her eyes again.

The screen was black.

She ran her finger over the pad again—still black.

Flipping it over and tapping on the bottom as all technically savvy people do, she arrived at a simple explanation: dead battery. The green power light was off; the fan was not running; the problem was easily fixed.

Standing, she walked back to the kitchen in a controlled but quick pace. Glancing at the desk, she saw no signs of the power cord. She ticked through the things she had used the laptop for, and then retraced her activities through the house.

She'd typed up the agenda for the meeting in her bed last night, but no cord there; sent an e-mail for work while drinking coffee that morning on the back porch, but no cord there either. Solicitation e-mails for donors in the war room, formerly known as the dining room; no cord there. She'd printed everything for the meeting in her office, but there was no cord there. That rounded out her list. Noah had been using the laptop to play games on the desk, and on the floor in her room, but it wasn't there, either. But that gave her an idea.

Entering her son's room, she went directly to the basket where he kept everything that had anything to do with his video games. There, nestled among the game cases, was the cord for his Nintendo DS, the very thing he had raced back into the house to get when his father had picked him up. In his rush, he must have taken the laptop cord instead.

Now Riley had a choice to make. She could wait until Noah returned the next day and read Sam's e-mail then, or she could call Daniel and see if he minded her coming to get the cord. The thought of rocking the boat with her ex was less then thrilling, but she needed to read that e-mail. The suspense was killing her, not to mention the fact that Noah would need his own charger at some point.

She flipped open her cell phone and called Daniel. Getting his voice mail, she left a quick message and tried to ignore her disappointment. Sighing, she tried to remember what exactly she had planned to do with her evening before this whole ordeal began. It was too late for a run. She considered ordering a movie on pay-per-view or just channel surfing, but she needed something to calm her.

Wandering back into her bedroom and then restlessly into the bathroom, she spied just the thing: a hot bath. It would relax her, take the chill out of the air, and give her a chance to get a handle on this whole Sam mess. She turned the spigots and dumped in some bath beads as the hot water filled the tub, releasing a scent of lavender, and she could feel the tension in her shoulders relax. She slipped out of her clothes and was just about to slide into the water when the doorbell rang, snapping her out of her relaxing state and right into "Who in the heck could that be?"

She grabbed her ratty robe and pulled it on as she headed toward the door. Nothing about this night was going as she intended, and glancing out the window, she could see that trend would continue. Daniel stood on her front step.

"Daniel, what are you doing here?" she asked, opening the door and trying to ignore the once-over he gave her. She pulled her robe a bit tighter and waited for his reply.

"I got your message about the cord and thought I'd run over and exchange it." He held it up as though it were proof as to what he was saying.

"I left that message, like, ten minutes ago," she puzzled. "How'd you get here so quickly?"

"We were at Tower Pizza with my sister. Noah's going over there for a bit, because I wanted to talk to you about something."

"Well, now's not a great time for me," she said slowly, thinking of both her bath getting colder by the second and that the arrival of the power cord meant she could read Sam's e-mail.

"I made a mistake, Riley," Daniel said quickly, as if he knew this might be his one opportunity. "I want to come back home to Noah, and to you."

Shaken, Riley stared at him blankly. No, this evening was definitely not turning out as she'd planned.

Chapter Nineteen

I have no response to that."

That was Riley's answer as her soon-to-be ex-husband stood on her doorstep, uttering the very words she had dreamed for months he would say. Aside from her ratty old robe with the missing belt, the cookie crumbs on her face, and the desire to run him off as soon as possible so she could read the e-mail from Sam, it was exactly how she pictured his mea culpa.

Her mind was muddled with what he'd done to her, who she'd become without him, and what she really wanted her life to be.

"No response?" He looked confused.

Riley shook her head. "Nope, no idea what you want me to say, or what I should say. This is a little unexpected, you have to admit."

"No, not really. We had a life, a family, and I screwed up. I want to come back and make it up to you." He looked at her intently, his eyes warm and familiar.

For a brief second, Riley caught a flash of the husband he had been. As angry as his leaving had made her, there was something about that look. And he was right about one thing: they'd had a life together, a son, and because of that she owed him and this pronouncement some thought, at the very least.

As tangled as her mind was, she knew that to be the truth, so she took a deep breath and let it out in a big sigh before replying. "I need to think about it."

It wasn't much, but apparently it was enough. His face filled with optimism.

"Okay. Well, then, I guess I'll go, so you can think." He smiled almost shyly and turned and walked down the driveway, slowly, glancing back as though he wanted to say more, plead his case, but then thought better of it.

Riley watched him go, but she doubted her own sincerity. She wasn't going to do much thinking about it in the near future, because all she wanted to do was use the power cord he had dropped off and read Sam's e-mail.

Reclaiming her computer from the living room couch, she hurried back to her room, plugged it in, and powered it up. She glanced around the dark room, the scent of lavender coming from her still full but surely now cold bathtub, the dance of the candles casting their moving shadows on her wall. Candles that had just minutes earlier made her think of relaxation but that now, ironically, spoke to her more intimate and romantic side. She thought about the night Sam had come over for her to vent about Trish, how he'd listened intently, played devil's advocate, and pushed her hair out of her eyes, his fingers brushing her forehead. A shiver went through her.

Riley again had to wonder when life was going to quit throwing her for a loop. Was it because for so long she'd been living by rote? Was that the lesson she was meant to learn? Pay attention?

Well, she was more than paying attention now.

She glanced down at the computer to see that the e-mail was up on her screen. A part of her wondered if she was making a bigger deal out of it than it was. After all, she was the one with the feelings for Sam. Nothing he had done would indicate that they were reciprocated. But then she recalled the tone of his message, and her heart fluttered once more. Anger at his dishonesty be damned, against her better judgment she couldn't wait to know what was so important it couldn't wait for a live conversation.

She clicked on the e-mail. It opened wide on the screen, and she began to read.

Riley,

As I said earlier, I hate to use e-mail to convey a message that is so important to me, but at this point, with my unexpected trip, the business of everyday life, and my urgent need to get this off my chest, I had no other option. I just want you to know up front that I would have rather told you this in person, or at the very least over the phone.

I have not been honest with you about my marriage, and though it is no excuse, I want you to know that it was for Max that I misled you. Writing it, I can see what a cop-out it sounds like, but it is the truth.

I was married to the most wonderful woman in the world. Together, we built a life and had a son. I intended to live out my days with her, but fate did not share the same vision for my life. My wonderful wife died three years ago, and I fully planned to spend my remaining days devoted to her memory and to my son. Until I met you. No one was more shocked by my attraction to you than I was. And I don't mean that in a bad way. You are a smart, beautiful, completely engaging woman. But the thing is, up until the moment you pulled me into that closet the first time we met, I still considered myself a married man. And I was so shocked by my interest in you. It felt like a betrayal. And then Max came to me and asked if we could keep his mother's death a secret. For the first time since his mom died, he wasn't dealing with the stigma of being the kid with the dead mom. He was just Max, the new kid in town, making friends, and he was happy, so I agreed. I see now that part of that agreement was so I could rationalize both spending time with you and ignoring my obvious attraction. I was scared.

None of that is an excuse for leading you to be-

lieve my wife was still alive, for lying to you. But I hope you will understand that I was honoring my son's wishes and sorting out my feelings. Maybe none of this matters. You are dealing with your own personal difficulties. Maybe a relationship with me is the farthest from your mind. And that would be fine, but something in your avoidance of my calls leads me to believe otherwise.

Again, I know dishonesty isn't something that sits well with you, but I hope you can understand my motivation. I look forward to hearing your reply, whatever it might be.

Sam

Riley stared at the e-mail, working parts of it over in her mind. She was numbed by the two confessions she'd heard that night and not at all sure what she thought or felt about either of them.

Chapter Twenty

I can do this, Riley thought to herself, smiling at Noah as he raced from her side and into the open arms of his father.

They were meeting Daniel at the park, a small gesture on her part after his confession a few nights before. He had called to see if the three of them could spend the sunny fall afternoon together, and she had no reason not to. Plus, she thought it might help to give her some perspective.

What could it hurt? She didn't have to buy into the whole happy family thing just because she had agreed to spend the afternoon together. At least that was what she was telling herself.

"There's my best guy!" Daniel exclaimed as Noah threw himself into his father's arms, an action that he was maybe a bit too old for, but that didn't seem to faze the boy in the least.

It was one of the things that Riley knew put a check

in her reconciliation column. Noah's happiness. It was important, but was it enough?

"Riley, thanks for agreeing to this," Daniel said, an earnest smile on his face. And, she had to admit, it sent a small flutter through her chest. Was it real? Nostalgia? The thrill of knowing he wanted her back after he had so carelessly tossed her aside? Time would tell, and it was part of the reason she had agreed to spend the day together.

Hanging his arm around Noah's shoulder, Daniel motioned for her to follow him away from the playground and toward the open field of the park. Riley tugged at the zipper of her down vest. The sky was a perfect blue, but when the breeze blew the thin clouds over the sun, the chill in the air was enough to make her wish she'd brought a scarf, and maybe even a hat, as she had done for Noah.

Riley couldn't help but take note of how Daniel was dressed—head to toe in a nylon track suit that almost squeaked when he walked. He was wearing shiny new sneakers and a turtleneck, all in coordinating bright blue and black. It occurred to her that he was dressed similarly to the women of the Hubbard School PTA, their sporty look. She smiled to herself at the thought of him gathered around the table at Coffee Chic with them prior to their exercise classes. He really did fit their mold better than she ever would.

"I hope you didn't eat," Daniel said as they made their way across the field and toward the edge of the woods that lined the back part of the field. "I took the liberty of putting together a little picnic."

Riley was slightly surprised to see that there was, in fact, a checked blanket, a basket, and a small vase of flowers laid out at the edge of the woods, set apart from the rest of the people using the park that day. Oddly, this blatant gesture caused not another flutter, but a wave of embarrassment. He was trying a bit too hard. And while she knew she should appreciate the effort, something about it seemed forced. But Riley had never been the kind of girl who went all in for the romantic gesture—she was more practical than that. And Daniel knew it.

One check in the "no reconciliation" column.

This was going to be a very long afternoon if she continued to treat it like a scorecard. But in her ever-swirling mind, she found it hard to turn it off.

So, instead, she settled cross-legged on the blanket next to her son and across from Daniel. Forcing a smile, she watched as he dove into the oddly perfect picnic basket and began unloading it before them.

For Noah there was a bologna sandwich, corn chips, apples with caramel sauce for dipping, a can of fruit punch and a bag of cookies. Noah's eyes danced at the can; seeing as how he wasn't allowed to drink soda, anything that even resembled it made him ecstatic. Riley was pleased to see that even though they were no longer living in the same house, the rules still applied.

Having provided for their son, Daniel turned his attention on her and just as swiftly produced a veritable feast that consisted of warm bread, brie, cut apples, thinly sliced prosciutto, and a thermos of warm apple cider.

"I thought about adding a little bit of cinnamon brandy, like we used to do before Noah, but then thought better of it," he said, smiling proudly at the wonderful food he had laid before her.

It did all look delicious, and it was thoughtful; Riley had to give him that. Feeling just a bit guilty for dismissing the picnic as a cheesy romantic ploy, she couldn't ignore his attention to the details of their lunch. Daniel always had been a great cook.

As she spread brie onto the warm bread, topping it with the apple and the salty ham, Riley thought of the Hamburger Helper she'd prepared for dinner the night before. She couldn't help but imagine going back to the hot, delicious meals that Daniel always had at the ready when they lived in the same house. She missed them. She missed the practical things he took care of in her life. But did she miss *him*?

Riley ate in relative silence, savoring the food and listening as Noah and Daniel took turns making up stories about the other people in the park. It was a game the three of them had played regularly on days just like this, seeing who could come up with the most outrageous fantasy life for the man jogging by in shorts and a tank top on this brisk fall day.

"He's a spy from some island country where it's

never cold. And he must have been sick the day the change of seasons was discussed in spy school." Noah giggled as he dunked his apple happily into his caramel dip.

"Or maybe he's using the old 'the more you stick out and seem crazy, the less likely anyone is to pay attention to you' ploy," Daniel added. "That's the oldest trick in the book for anyone who knows anything about spies."

"And you two know a lot about spies," Riley said, wiggling her finger into Noah's rib.

"Mom, we've only seen *Spy Kids* a zillion times. No one knows more about spies and spy school than me and Daddy."

"That is true, little man," Daniel said, winking at Riley over the boy's head.

Flutter.

It was faint, but a flutter nonetheless. Riley sighed, not sure how she was ever going to sort through the mess of thoughts and emotions.

So, instead, she picked out a young woman who was dressed oddly in wide-striped leggings, a bulky, belted sweater, and a beret pushing an old-fashioned pram. "Well, don't look now, but I think someone just might be onto your warm-weather spy," she said, pointing in the woman's direction.

"Yeah, nobody uses that kind of stroller anymore," Daniel concurred.

"I bet it's full of satellite equipment," added Noah.

And the three of them giggled at the convoluted story they had just created. She was enjoying herself; even in her confused state, Riley had to admit that.

She glanced around the park and wondered how many people walking by would see them laughing on their blanket and take them for just another happy family enjoying the beautiful day. And wasn't that what they were, at least in that moment? Riley didn't know.

"Who's up for some Frisbee?" Daniel asked, pulling the orange disc out of the bottom of the basket.

"Me! I am!" Noah jumped up and grabbed it from his father's hand, then raced into the open field.

"You two go ahead. I'll clean all this up real quick. Maybe we can go give the rest of this bread to the ducks at the pond before they all fly south for the winter?"

"Sounds like a plan to me." Daniel stood up to follow Noah but took the time to turn and run backwards so that he could once again shoot her a smile full of gratitude.

That darn perfect smile was, frankly, one of the reasons she had agreed to go out with him in the first place. But he'd need more than just a smile to send her running back this time.

She sighed as she began placing lids on the containers and putting them back in the basket. Then she gathered up the trash and headed out in search of a garbage can. Finding none near the walking path or the dog park, she headed toward the restroom.

"Why in the world would they put so few trash cans

in such a big park?" she muttered to herself, surveying the scene in search of one.

Finally she spied a large green receptacle near the back of the restroom, its lid covered in something black and stuck open due to the vast amounts of garbage shoved inside. Riley readjusted her own pile of garbage and tried to figure out just how she was going to throw any of it away without getting the mystery goo on her hands.

"Looks like you could use a hand." The warm, familiar voice stopped her mid–garbage dump. And she knew, without looking, that the tinge of humor in his voice would come with a sparkle in his clear blue eyes.

Sam.

From behind her, he reached around and pushed up the open lid enough so that she could deposit her trash.

Her heart pounded, not fluttered. Pounded. Fast and strong enough that the sound of her own pulse drowned out whatever he said next. She turned to look at him, and the contrast to Daniel was apparent.

Sam's smile was true, almost bashful. He wore no flashy, trendy sport clothes. Just clothes that were comfortable and reliable, like Sam himself had been.

Except that he had misled her, lied to her. She had yet to reply to his e-mail. The one that explained it all away, apologized but justified his actions. Did it excuse the dishonesty? Riley hadn't been sure, which was why she hadn't replied. And now here she was at the park with Daniel and Noah, trying to feel like reuniting her family was the way to go but not quite sure about that either.

All of these thoughts flooded her mind. Her pulse raced and her face flushed, and Riley was at a loss as to what she was supposed to do. Looking at him, his head tilted ever so slightly, her mind clouded by so many thoughts and emotions, Riley did something that surprised even her.

She stepped toward him, quickly, and kissed him. His mouth warm on hers, he welcomed her into his arms, pulling her closer. And for just a second she was calm.

Until, that is, she realized what she was doing. Embarrassed, she pulled away. "Sam, I can't believe I did that," she stammered, her eyes still locked on his, relieved for the most part to see there was no look of amusement or mocking there.

Instead, she found the same sweet expression on his face, and her already-flushed face flooded with heat.

"It wasn't exactly the greeting I was expecting, not that I'm complaining or anything," he said, his smile sincere and not a hint of sarcasm in his voice. "You never did reply to my e-mail."

"I know. I know. There's just so much going on. Daniel wants to reconcile. You're sending me confession e-mails. I'm so confused. I'm sorry, but I . . ." She faltered, her mind flashing with the images of her son happily playing with his father. She was at the park with them, and she'd kissed Sam, whom she wasn't even sure she had forgiven.

Riley Andrews was not the kind of woman who kissed a man out of confusion. Had she lost even her thin grasp of reality?

"I have to go. I'm sorry."

His expression changed to one of disappointment.

"That you have to go, or that you kissed me?"

Riley turned, unable to answer because she wasn't sure. But as she walked away, her heart still pounded, her lips could still feel the sweet pressure of his, and the one thing she knew for certain was that the flutter she felt for Daniel didn't compare.

What she wished more than anything was to have a moment to collect herself. As she neared the spot where just minutes earlier she had been having a picnic with her family, however, she could see that not only would there be no moment for her, but the ante had been raised.

Standing there, talking to Daniel, were the last people she'd want to run into on a good day—Cupcake and Screamer. Their too-enthusiastic voices were raised to a pitch she was sure would bring all the dogs from the park running. Riley considered turning on her heel, but it was too late. They'd spotted her.

"Riley! Daniel was just telling us the good news!" Cupcake squealed, and before Riley had even a second to process, Screamer answered the very question she'd been forming.

"A reconciliation! How wonderful! We all win—you can go back to work, and we can get this handsome man back into the Hubbard School PTA!"

Riley knew the expression on her face wasn't appropriate, but she couldn't help it. She was dumbfounded.
The only saving grace was that Noah was still tossing
the Frisbee out of earshot. She stared at Daniel, who
shot her a toothy grin. But this time there was no flutter.
No, this time all she felt was irritation, and a deep desire to remove that smile from his face.

Chapter Twenty-one

Shopping? Are you kidding me? With all that I have left to do, you want me to go shopping?"

But yet here she was, standing in the middle of the Nordstrom formal dress section with her sister, thumbing mindlessly through racks of black cocktail dresses. Her sister, having disappeared to find Topher, the salesman, to check on some designer shipment that had been expected but not yet delivered. Topher, according to Trish, was the new nickname for Christopher, the trendier, hipper version. Who knew there were hip nicknames in the suburbs?

As much as there was to do, Riley still couldn't convince her sister she'd meant it when she said she had no time for shopping. And, for that matter, that she didn't really care what she wore to this gala. She was sure Trish may have interpreted the word *no* to mean the exact opposite. In the end, it was just easier to carve out a few hours and go than to keep fending off the phone calls.

And it did give her something to do, to keep her from

bouncing around like one of those SuperBalls that Noah loved. Sam, Daniel, new life, old life, single mom, working mom, stay-at-home mom, new relationship, old relationship, settling, taking a chance, none of the above— it was like a constant strain of thoughts that rambled through her mind any time she wasn't busy doing something else. And at this point, it all just bounced around, arriving at no conclusion.

She kept replaying the scene at the park in her head, like dueling scenarios of what her life could be. The flashes of good in both, but just as easily the parts that didn't sit well with her—like Daniel telling the PTA-ers they were reconciling or Sam reappearing without telling her he was back. And Noah, always Noah, with his happy smile, holding tight to his parents' hands as he walked between them to the car. Life should not be this hard.

Daniel's apology for his misrepresentation to her enemies.

Bounce, bounce, bounce.

Sam's relaxed reaction to her throwing herself at him.

Bounce, bounce, bounce.

She was sort of getting used to the constant hum in her brain, and that wasn't a good thing. Just days ago, hadn't she thought she had her life under control? But that was before these men had decided to reappear with their confessions.

Hence the shopping trip. A distraction, some QT with her sister, and she needed a new dress, or so she'd been told.

"It's still not here. I'm not sure why. They always get the Nicole Miller winter line in time for the Winter Gala." Trish had returned without Riley knowing it, and she jumped at the sound of her sister's voice.

"Bummer," she said, not sure what the appropriate response was to such a statement.

"Isn't it?" Her sister faked a pout and then a broad smile stretched across her perfectly glossed lips. "Lucky for me, I already bought a backup when I was in New York last month."

"If you already have a dress, why are we here?" Part of Trish's reason for the shopping trip was her need to find something that wouldn't show Riley up as the chair of the event. A dress that would accent her sister "like a great pair of heels or the right earrings," whatever that meant. She said it using her fingers as air quotes, which was apparently supposed to serve as a translation. But as with the hip new nickname for Christopher, Riley didn't get it.

"Well, it certainly isn't to look at these drab things!" Trish exclaimed a bit too dramatically, dismissing the entire rack of dresses Riley had been browsing through with a flick of her French manicure. "Follow me."

"I like these. They're black. You can never lose with a simple black cocktail dress," Riley argued, though she followed Trish through the maze of racks away from the very dresses she was championing.

"You're right, but sometimes you can't win with one, either." She said it so assuredly that for some ridiculous reason, Riley felt as though finding the perfect dress would be the solution to all her problems.

If only.

"Again, why are you shopping for a dress if you already have one?"

"Because *you* don't," Trish quipped over her shoulder. She continued her march through the racks, her voice a combination of determination and expertise that Riley had grown accustomed to in the past few weeks. And when she used it, Riley had to admit, Trish was usually right.

"I'm not conceding the black dress," she retorted, though without much conviction. The business world had taught her that sometimes letting an expert handle details in their field of expertise was a good thing. With all Riley had on her plate, turning over her dress choice to her sister was looking better and better.

Ahead of her Trish stopped dead in her tracks, turned ever so slowly, and delicately plucked a dress from the very back of the rack she had stopped in front of.

"This is the one."

Amazed that her sister had snatched the thing from the obscurity of the crowded rack, Riley couldn't control her eye roll.

"First of all, it can't be the right size. Second, how can you possibly even know that based on the smidge of it you could see as you walked by? And third, I am not wearing yellow."

All were true enough reasons, but the yellow was really

the kiss of death as far as Riley was concerned. She'd had to wear a yellow robe for eighth-grade graduation, and because of her height she had earned the nickname Big Bird from her fellow graduates. The nickname had stuck well through high school in certain circles and had even found its way into her senior yearbook. She'd been emotionally scarred and had sworn off wearing the color for life.

Trish stared at her, a hard and serious look, but Riley met her gaze with equal intensity until her sister looked away. Her heart fluttered with victory until a calm and cool Trish answered with her own list.

"Size 8. It isn't yellow; it's umber. And it is the dress, because I *know* it is. Period. Now go and try it on." She held it out with one hand and put the other on her hip.

Riley had to admit, yellow or umber aside, it was a gorgeous dress. And there was the whole letting-experts-do-what-they-do-best philosophy she'd been working with for the entire event. Reluctantly, she grabbed the hanger from her sister and walked past her toward the dressing rooms.

"Stay close. I'm not going to wander around the store looking for you in this thing," she said, ignoring the smile on Trish's face.

Back in the dressing room, she pulled off her fleece sweatshirt and jeans, grateful that she'd had the sense to put on one of her good bras for this excursion. She'd taken to keeping her sports bra on so that she could get in a workout whenever she had time. It helped relieve the stress. With this neckline, a sports bra would have been more than obvious to her sister, who would have gone ballistic at Riley's lack of preparation, or commitment, or whatever.

She slipped the dress off the hanger and over her head, and the soft fabric settled around her body effortlessly. Trish was right. It was the perfect dress.

She pulled the zipper up under her arm and then turned to look at her reflection in the mirror. Even with the soft-effect lighting in the Nordstrom dressing room, Riley could tell that there was something about the dress that suited her exactly.

The bottom was an umber silk that seemed to darken in the creases. It was cut to the knee and hugged her hips. The skirt flowed from an empire waist that gathered just below her bust, where the color deepened and was accented by delicate, rust-colored sequins. The warm colors brought out the flecks of gold in her eyes and the streaks of auburn in her hair. And the halter of the top showed the muscular curve of her shoulders and the delicate line of her collarbone.

It was an exquisite dress. Somehow, it managed to make Riley feel more feminine and beautiful than she had felt in a year. The only moment that even came close had been when Sam had tucked a lock of hair behind her ear that night at her kitchen table.

Thinking of that, and looking at herself in the mirror, the bouncing ball stopped.

Finally, Riley knew, as clearly as the mirror displayed

her reflection, what she wanted. She wanted to stand on her own two feet. Run her own life. Make her own way in this new world she'd been thrust into. And she wanted Sam to be there laughing with her and supporting her as she did it.

She was falling in love with Sam.

His dishonesty had been for the best of reasons—his son. She could forgive him that. After all, she'd been entertaining the notion of taking back her ex-husband for the very same one. It was one of the things they had in common, one of the things she respected the most about him. That he would do anything for his son.

"Hello in there? Are you going to come out and show me how right I am?"

Riley stepped out from behind the curtains—floated, really. Not even the knowing look on her sister's face could dampen the elation she felt at having finally calmed her inner demons.

"Trish, I will never doubt you when it comes to fashion again."

Something in her sister's face softened, and the result seemed to wipe away the carefully applied makeup and erase the faint lines around her eyes. Trish looked much as she had when they were girls.

"Riley, you look exquisite."

"I kind of do! I can say that, since it's only true because you made me put this dress on." Inside, Riley's heart tugged for her sister. "You know, Trish, I didn't give you enough credit before, for all that you do, and how well you do it. You're pretty amazing at this way of life."

Trish's eyes flooded. "You have no idea how long I've wanted my older, professional, successful sister to say such a thing."

"Well, it shouldn't have taken me so long to say what I've always thought. I never could have pulled any of this off without you—the PTA, the gala, even this perfect dress. I know I fought kicking and screaming the entire time, but I really can't think of a way that I will ever be able to thank you."

Trish smiled warmly. "My thanks will be you going to your gala, in this dress, and showing everyone just how successful my big sister is."

It dawned on Riley that Sam had been right. All the clashes they'd had over the years had been about respect, not about who was doing things the right way. Funny that it had taken someone completely new to the situation to come up with the answer.

In her life, Riley thought, she was going to need more of that. She sighed, smiled at Trish, and knew, deep down, that it was all going to work out for her. Maybe not as she'd planned, but it will work out for the best nonetheless.

Epilogue

The night was perfect. Around her the room was filled with people opening up their wallets and buying up the auction items that had, as Trish predicted, magically appeared. The live jazz band played softly in the background. The scents of the gourmet appetizers wafted into the air as white-gloved waiters passed through the crowd offering them up on silver trays.

Riley stood at the back, surveying the crowd. Her sense of accomplishment was equaled only by the thrill that she'd pulled the whole thing together on her own terms in the end. And it seemed to be going off without a hitch.

As if on cue, a gaggle of the PTA regulars approached, their faces plastered with smiles that reminded her of the jack-o'-lanterns that just a month ago had lined the porches of her neighborhood.

"Riley, I must admit I was leery of your delegating, but it seems to be working."

Riley knew it was as close to a compliment or thank-you as she was ever going to receive, and sometimes you had to take whatever small victory you could. "Thank you, Stephanie Ann. I'm just glad we're raising some money for the school." She hoped it was enough of an answer to keep the group of them moving, but that was not to be.

"So, I heard about you and Daniel," Cupcake said, leaning in as if to make the conversation more intimate, though she actually seemed to be speaking louder. "So sorry you couldn't patch up your differences." She nodded her head toward the other end of the room, where Riley could see Daniel, smiling broadly, surrounded by a group of women.

"I appreciate that, but, really, it's for the best," Riley replied, modeling her response as coyly as she could, and just as loud.

"So, if Daniel is coming back to the ranks of our PTA, I guess that lets you off the hook."

Riley smiled back, as sweetly as the catty comment had been said. "Luckily, you won't have to choose. You're getting us both."

They stared blankly at her, and Riley bit her lip to keep from laughing at their attempts to contain their disappointment. She was staying in the Hubbard School PTA, and she'd been able to reconfigure her schedule so she could be a full-time ad executive too. It was all falling into place.

Her son was happy. Her life was rewarding, and thankfully, the bouncing in her head had all but stopped.

"In the end, it seems Riley has found the PTA most

enjoyable." His voice enveloped the group as surely as his arm that went around her waist. And as rewarding as it was to have put together a successful gala on her own terms, it didn't compare to the shocked looks that appeared on their faces as she slid her own arm around Sam's waist.

She turned and smiled up at him, and in the moment saw only him. She turned ever so slightly, and he bent and kissed her lightly on the lips, but even that was enough to add a zip to her pulse.

"And we are really lucky to have such a smart, professional woman giving us a new perspective."

Riley pulled back from Sam and found herself staring at the broad smile of Annie.

"As successful as this event is, just think about what she could do next," Annie continued, heaping on the compliments that Riley knew were more about sticking it to the PTA posse than praising her.

"I can't imagine."

"Of course."

The mumbled responses were without enthusiasm, and the looks on their faces spoke of their desire to run away and talk mercilessly about it all.

Riley smiled the confident, calm smile she had managed to reclaim in the past week. And then she gave them one last thing to discuss. One last thing that would send *them* spinning for a change.

"Actually, I'm thinking of running for Hubbard School PTA president next year."